USA TODAY BESTSELLING AUTHOR
Dale Mayer

Johan's
JOY

HEROES FOR HIRE

JOHAN'S JOY: HEROES FOR HIRE, BOOK 21
Dale Mayer
Valley Publishing Ltd.

Copyright © 2020

ISBN-13: 978-1-773363-52-3
Print Edition

Books in This Series:

About This Book

After helping out Vince, Johan hadn't planned on staying at Levi and Ice's compound for long. However, Johan realizes how much plans can change when Galen comes over from Africa to join Johan, and the two are sent into town on a job that's close and up-front personal to another member of Legendary Security.

Joyce, otherwise called Joy, sought a career position but accepted something out of her normal skill set in order to pay the rent. But when her inventory lists show missing drugs, she knows something ugly is going on. With no one at the company willing to listen, she turns to her old friend Kai for advice.

Johan wasn't the answer Joy was looking for, but, when she finds out the previous employee to hold her position is in the morgue, she's damn happy to have him.

Her job might be safe ... but her life? Well, that's on the line ...

Sign up to be notified of all Dale's releases here!
https://smarturl.it/DaleNews

Chapter 1

JOHAN KOTTON WALKED through the compound's huge kitchen area, snagged a cinnamon bun, and poured himself a cup of coffee, then wandered into the adjoining room, where a large group sat around the dining room table, talking. As he took the last seat, Kai looked over at him, grinned, and said, "You'll get fat here if you keep eating like that."

Johan nodded sagely. "You could be right," he said, "but I'll worry about it later. These are too damn good to miss out on."

"Those are Bailey's cinnamon buns," Kai said. "They're to die for."

He munched his way through it, thoroughly enjoying the different tastes of everything over here. He had traveled for years in his work, decades even, but he had spent the last five years with Bullard over in Africa, until Johan had been sent off the Galápagos Islands to help rescue a science team. He'd come back, along with Galen Alrick, to Ice and Levi's compound in the outskirts of Houston for a week or two. He was hoping to do a mission or two here and see just how different it was.

He was originally from the US, but his parents had been missionaries and had traveled all over the world. He'd gone to school in England and in Michigan. School hadn't really stuck, and he'd gone on to working in various trades in Germany and then in Switzerland. It was hard, as he looked back through his vagabond lifestyle, to place any area as home.

As he pondered the cinnamon bun in this strange path his world had taken, he heard Kai say, "I know, but it's Joy, and she's not one much for raising the alarm."

"You know Joy. We don't," Harrison said. "And she might not be one to raise alarms, but that doesn't mean she's not making this a bigger deal than it is."

Kai shrugged, sank back in her chair and said, "I think you're wrong."

"What did I miss out on?" Johan asked, as he took another bite of his cinnamon bun.

Kai turned toward him. "A friend of mine, Joy—well, it's actually *Joyce*, but we've always called her Joy," Kai said. "She's working at the corporate office for a medical research center and says a mess of drugs are missing from her inventory."

"Drugs are always missing," Johan said. "I swear it goes along with every medical center I've ever seen."

"I agree," she said, "but, in this case, it's knockout drugs."

He raised an eyebrow. "Are those a hot commodity on the black market here?"

"Yes," Harrison said. "Unfortunately. And, in this case, the drug is ketamine, which is what they use to knock out horses."

"Or men," Johan said quietly. "We've had serial killers using that same drug before."

"I never thought about a serial killer," Kai said, her eyes round as she stared at him. "And I definitely won't mention it to Joy."

He chuckled. "No need to really put the panic into her. Besides, if it's just one or two bottles, is that something everybody's worried about, or is it a much bigger issue?"

"She's new there," Kai said. "She was hired by Westgroup as the inventory clerk, working in their corporate offices, which includes their oversight of a large research center. The two buildings are near each other on the same block, I believe. They don't do any animal testing, but they're doing a lot of work on various animals, so they knock them out to do surgeries."

"Sounds like animal testing to me," Johan said, as the last bite of the cinnamon bun went into his mouth.

"I hope not," Kai said darkly. "It would make Joy very unhappy."

"What's the difference between animal testing and experimental surgery?" he asked curiously.

"Motivation, I think," Harrison said, with a laugh.

"Either way," Kai said, "the corporate office is near the medical research facility which is run alongside a large vet clinic, and, per Joy's inventory records, a lot of ketamine went missing."

"Nobody should stock a lot of ketamine," Johan said. "It's a very strong drug, and you don't need very much of it. So, unless they're dealing with a huge population of bovine, horses, or, say, elephants," he said with a snort, "I can't see anybody having a large stock of it."

"True enough, but they did get a large amount in, and now it's gone."

Johan stared at her, his fingers tapping away on his knees. His mind raced as he thought about all the uses for ketamine. "If it was a serial killer, he won't need a lot of ketamine anyway."

"But, like you said, it's worth money on the black market," Kai said. And then she turned to Harrison and frowned. "Wait. You said that."

"That was me," Harrison said with a nod. "But it doesn't matter. Drugs that go missing are an issue. Have they contacted the cops?"

"No. See? That's a funny thing. Joy said that she brought it up with her boss, and he just laughed at her, said she must have miscounted, so she should go back and do it again."

"Did she?" Johan asked, interested in the way the system worked over here. Africa was a whole lot more lax in some ways because you could be staring down the barrel of a rifle pretty damn fast. So Africa had less of a certain type of crime because the on-the-spot punishment would be so much more severe. But Johan had done many jobs in Europe, and even in the US too, and he knew that things were on a much different scale here.

"She did, indeed, and, when she went back to him, he said it must have been an inventory error."

"Did she go to their accountant over it?"

Kai looked at Harrison and nodded. "The accountant wasn't happy and commented that the stuff was expensive but didn't confirm whether he had entered an invoice for a case of ketamine or not."

"Sounds like she's trying to do the right thing and to track it down, but nobody else seems to care."

"I think that's a problem for a lot of large companies," she said. "Because somebody else will end up taking the blame, if it did go missing."

"And is that our problem, or is this just a thought exercise that we're all talking about?" Johan asked.

"I dumped it in Ice's lap," Kai confessed. "So I'm not sure what she'll do with it. Considering the type of drugs we're talking about, I imagine she'll bring in the cops."

The steady *clip-clip* sound of footsteps coming down the hallway said they were about to find out. As Ice walked in, her hair in a long braid down her back, wearing a simple white flowing shirt over jeans and sandals, she looked as cool, calm, and collected as ever.

Johan had heard that she was pregnant, but she wasn't showing much, if at all, if that was the case.

Ice had on reading glasses and pulled them down her nose so she could see over them. "I spoke to Joy," she said. "She's really worried, but her section boss is apparently brushing it off."

"Yes, that's what she told me," Kai said.

Ice nodded. "However, I went several rungs higher on the ladder to somebody I know on the board."

"Of course you know somebody on the board," Kai said in a drawling voice. "Is there anybody here in Houston that you don't know?"

Ice flashed her bright grin. "It helps to know a lot of people, not only the local ones," she said. "I just had a private conversation with him, and he's not impressed. He said, whether it was a clerical error or a theft, it's not a drug they want to have floating around, particularly as the lot numbers would lead back to his company's research lab."

"Never thought of that," Kai said. "That gives more weight to getting this solved."

"Well, it should have been resolved right off the bat," Johan said.

Ice looked at him with interest. "You wanted to do a job,

right?"

He nodded immediately.

"Good," she said. "Then you and Galen can go."

At that, a silence hung around the place. Johan looked around and said, "And why is everybody all of a sudden staring at me that way?"

"You're not one of our regular guys, don't know the lay of the land here," Harrison said easily. He looked at Ice and said, "Don't you want one of us to go too?"

"You mean, besides Galen, who is also one of Bullard's men?"

Harrison gave a one-armed shrug. "Yeah. Like which streets to avoid and who to call at the police department. And which restaurants to avoid." He chuckled at his own joke.

She pondered it and said, "Well, I do have a job in the same area. I could send two of you over there, and, if these guys needed help, you could step up to aid them, and vice versa."

Harrison frowned but said, "I'm game. It's in Houston, isn't it?"

"Yes," she said. "And so is the other job."

"We don't get many jobs close together like that," he said. "What's the second job?"

"A large art theft," she said.

He stared at her in shock.

She shrugged. "What can I say? Apparently we're broadening our horizons."

"Please tell me it's something exotic, like involving an international jewel thief or something like that," he joked. "Sounds mundane to think of a local museum getting broken into."

"African sculptures," she said.

"So then we should do the Westgroup job and their stolen drugs," Harrison said, "and Galen and Johan should do the African sculpture job."

"Like I know anything about African sculptures," Johan joked.

Just then Galen walked into the area. He lifted a hand, walked over, and gave Ice a gentle hug, then tossed his bag on the floor, and dropped into a squatting position beside Johan. He grinned at his old friend. "Sounds like she's got a job for us."

"Oh, yeah. She's just trying to keep us together and away from her pretty boys," he said. "Everybody knows they can't handle the heat."

Galen burst into laughter. "Well, if they can't," he said, "I'm not sure anybody can." He stood and stretched. "Glad I'm here, though, man, that's a long set of flights to get here."

"It is, indeed," Ice said, staring at him. "We just got word that our men arrived there too."

"Yeah, Bullard's gnashing his teeth already," he said. "They've taken over some interesting security stuff. I wouldn't mind hearing what they're up to."

"Well, you can learn while you're here," she said. "In the meantime, Bullard wanted you to get some North American experience."

"So it's interesting that you're putting the two of us together," Galen said.

"Well, only because a job is right next door with a museum that had another kind of a theft. African art statues."

Galen rolled his eyes. "Art's not really my thing," he said, "unless shooting them up and leaving a room devastated is an art form."

"We have more than enough of that art form ourselves," she said in a mocking tone. "So, you two go to the ketamine theft, and I'll assign the art theft to another two guys."

"You know what? If the museum had only hired us in the first place as security," Harrison said, "they wouldn't have had an issue."

"Unfortunately," Ice said, "they are just now realizing that."

"So how major is this art theft?" Harrison asked.

"Well, it'll definitely be an issue between the two countries. The display was on loan from Nairobi," she said, "and they're very unhappy to know that four pieces have gone missing."

"Right," Harrison said, standing up and reaching over to shake Galen's hand in greeting. "So, me and who else?"

"Good question," she said, looking at her sheet. "I've got nine jobs in progress right now."

Harrison looked around. "I thought the place was pretty damn empty."

"Yeah, but I've got Tyson here. So maybe you and Tyson."

Harrison crossed his arms over his chest and nodded. "Pretty boy Tyson. He'll do just fine in a museum, but me, not so much."

"You'll do fine too," she said cheerfully, "because that's the job."

JOYCE BAXTER, OR Joy as she preferred to be called, stopped in her tracks, sighed deeply, and faced the mammoth building before her. It may look like one building, but it seemed to be two buildings sharing one common wall, in her mind. She worked in the corporate section, basically the front of the building on all the aboveground floors, even on some of the basement levels, like where her office was.

In the corporate world, the peons were given the windowless offices, reserving the window-filled penthouse offices for the CEOs, the owners, the board members. Those in-between positions got the offices on the in-between floors.

Regardless, she could enter the main entrance without setting off alarms. Supposedly the back of the building housed a portion of the research department and had its own entrance at the rear as well.

Even the elevators were segregated. One set in the front of the building was strictly designated for the office workers, with the other set for the researchers not even visible or reachable from any floor on the front side of the building.

Joy shook her head. She knew, per employee records, some 240 people were employed by the company. Yet Joy saw only a handful of those, all dressed in suits, in her section. Most of the employees seemed to work for the lab itself, which was in a separate building on the same block. Yet still a research department was in her building, but she had never seen evidence of it in her weeks of working here. She envisioned the researchers all wearing white lab coats, but what did she really know about this place? Maybe those researchers were more the evidence-gathering types, searching the web, wearing jeans and T-shirts. That would place the lab-coat guys at the actual lab itself down the road. Possibly.

She sighed again and walked into the building on one more Monday morning, already feeling the cramping tension going up her spine to the back of her neck. She'd been so happy to get this job, but now all she could think about was the fact that everybody was hiding something, and she hated it. She was very much a straightforward, up-front, easy-to-get-along-with kind of gal, but don't screw her around either. Now she felt like something was not quite right with her job, and nobody would talk to her about it.

How was she supposed to do her job if that was the case? It was frustrating, and she wasn't sure what the answer was. If there even was an answer. Half of her realized that this was all a big mess, and, having moved to town three months ago, she should have another job in her pocket already; yet it had taken her six weeks to find this one. Her sigh came out as a moan this time.

Using her security code to enter her floor, she walked in and headed to her back office in the dungeon level, grateful to find it empty. She normally shared it with two other women, who should arrive shortly. Joy dropped her sweater over the back of her chair, slipped her purse in her bottom drawer, sat down, and logged on to her computer. Except that, as soon as she brought up her screen, the log-in screen wasn't there, suggesting she was still logged in. As if she hadn't logged out on Friday.

She sank back in her chair, staring at the computer screen in horror. It was *possible* she hadn't logged out, but it certainly wasn't her normal procedure. Because that was against the security policy of the company. And the last thing she wanted to do was get fired, and, right now, this screen was not what she wanted to see.

She wasn't terribly techie oriented, but she figured there had to be a way to see if anybody had been on her computer over the weekend. But, when she tried to bring up documents, it seemed like only her own documents surfaced, just as she had last seen them. She brought up a web browser, but a lot of the pages were blocked normally anyway. She checked the browser history, but nothing seemed to be any different. Feeling relieved, but, at the same time, a little worried, she checked her email, but nothing terribly important was coming in either.

Still, it left her with an odd feeling. Like someone was checking up on her. She rose and headed to the break room to grab some coffee, hoping that some was made, because there wasn't always, and she ended up putting on a pot 90 percent of the time. But, of course, this early in the day on a Monday, there wasn't any made yet. As she stood here and looked out the small windows placed high in the wall—like a basement window in a house—she could see several other vehicles coming in. A couple hundred people worked at the company in various locations. They were developing drugs, and, although they supposedly weren't doing any tests on animals, it wasn't odd for Joy to travel to and from her parking spot and see a steady stream of animals coming through the main lab building, just down the block, getting treatments—special cases where owners were willing to test a new drug in order to save their furry family member. And, if Joy had been in that situation, then she'd try anything too.

Even if she were a human cancer patient, with some rare form of the disease, and somebody had a medical trial running, she would do everything she could to get that last chance too. It was hard to blame anybody who wanted to get their pets and other animals, much less their family, in on a special deal. How strange to think about that here, in the context of her new job in a new state. When she first took this job, she had hoped to never deal with death in any way.

She was technically an ER nurse but had burned-out

almost eighteen months ago now. After some of her friends had come in after a car crash one night, she had done everything she could to save them, but they both had passed away within twenty-four hours. She realized that all her nights of overtime and covering shifts on her days off had gradually resulted in her frequently working seven days a week, with long and highly stressful shifts. She had walked away and gone to jobs that didn't have the same emotional devastation.

The hospital had tried to get her to stay, but it had been almost impossible for her to even talk to her boss about the inciting event. When he realized she was too traumatized, he'd set her up with a therapist and had explained that he was completely okay with her doing whatever she needed to do to deal with this. She had thanked him and had attended the therapy sessions, initially doubting what they could do.

Yet, one of the best things she had done for her own soul and sanity was pick up a paintbrush through her art therapy appointments. It had taken her a long time to get out of the darker colors, and her therapist had been quite delighted with her progress, explaining that the dark colors were just evidence of the depression, dealing with the death that she had witnessed over and over and over again.

The words of her therapist rang in her ears. *Remember. Not everybody deals with death on a daily basis. As an ER nurse, you certainly did. You dealt with it more than most people do.* Those sessions had gone a long way to getting Joy back on her feet. She finally had to admit that, sometimes, death wins—even when Joy had done all she possibly could.

Her medical knowledge had given her a step up into this position in the pharmaceutical world. And here she was, after a year off, after finally landing this job, finding herself sitting here, looking down the barrel of a position that wasn't what she thought it would be.

If she hadn't discovered a missing case of ketamine in her paperwork, it wouldn't have been any big deal. She'd found other drugs unaccounted for as well, but it was like a bottle here or a syringe there. And stuff like that went missing from hospitals all the time. The administrators tried not to have missing inventory to explain, but it was almost impossible to keep track of every little thing, especially in the hectic ER environment. Saving the patient was paramount. Doing the paperwork? Not important on many levels.

But a whole case of ketamine? That bothered her. When the coffee was done, she poured herself a cup and slowly made her way back to her office. A few people had arrived, but not everybody all at once, and she was surprised at that. James, her boss, appeared at the front door to her office, just as she was passing through.

"Did you have a good weekend?" he asked with a smile.

"Excellent, thank you," she said in a cheerful voice.

He looked around as he took off his jacket and threw it over his shoulder. "Hardly anybody's here yet. What's up with that?"

"I know a lot of heavy traffic is downtown," she said, "so, depending on what route they're traveling, this one could be bad for anybody getting in on time."

His expression clearly said he doubted that suggestion, but he nodded. "That could be it. Otherwise it's lazy Monday attendees, and we've gone a long way to stop that from happening." With a frown, he turned and left.

She rushed to her desk, grateful that he didn't know she had walked in a couple minutes behind schedule too. She didn't want to make a bad impression because this could turn out to be a great job. And maybe the problem was her. After all that time off getting her shit together, it didn't seem like she *was* together, and this job was looking to be more onerous than she had thought. She was looking for something stress-free, where she could show up and put in her hours, get a paycheck, and go home with none of this on her mind.

Just as Joy sat down, one of the other women came rushing in, as if she were late.

Doris looked at the clock on the wall across the room. "No matter how hard I try," she said, "I'm always five minutes late."

Joy looked back at the clock to see it was 8:05 a.m. "Sorry," she said.

"And you're always early," the woman replied.

"I thought I was a couple minutes late this morning," she said. "At least I thought the other clock said so."

"They do that on purpose," Doris snapped. "The one in the main hall is set forward a little bit to keep everybody racing, as if they're behind."

"Well, we're definitely behind on some things in here," Joy said, "but that is a dirty trick with the clock." She'd have to remember that.

She brought up her email again and found a couple things she needed to deal with. With those done, she returned to the project she had been working on last Friday and dove back in. She wondered if her conversation with Kai would bear any fruit because that missing case of ketamine definitely bothered Joy. But, if Kai gets in trouble over it, then Joy didn't want Kai to deal with it either. Joy hadn't been working for more than fifteen minutes when her phone buzzed. She picked it up and answered. Her section boss,

James, ordered her to his office. He hung up before she had a chance to even respond.

Slowly she put down the receiver, grabbing paper and pen. She stood, wondering if she should grab her purse and her sweater too, and headed to her boss's office.

As she walked into James's office, he frowned at her. "I don't know what your connection is, and it would have been nice if you had told me in the first place," he snapped. "We don't like employees keeping stuff secret from the bosses."

She frowned at him. "I don't know what you're talking about."

He motioned behind her at two men she didn't recognize. One reached out his hand and introduced himself as Johan and said the other one was Galen. Just then a third guy walked in, happy and bustling.

"Good, good, good. Everybody arrived."

Her boss immediately stood to attention. "Sir?"

"These men are here at my request," he said.

Confusion crossed her boss's face. "I don't understand."

James looked at her, and she shrugged. "Don't look at me."

"Not at all," the new arrival said, as he reached out a hand. "I'm Edward Thornton." He introduced himself to Joy, as she shook his hand. "I'm on the board and have decided to open up an investigation into our inventory issues," he said with a warm smile.

She was dumbfounded. She didn't know if this was a result of her questions to Kai and wondered if she could even make something like this happen so fast. Joy didn't understand.

Edward motioned her to the chair. "Sit down, sit down."

She dropped in place, rather than sitting ladylike.

Johan and Galen stood off to the side, their arms crossed over their chests. They looked more like private security than investigators, but maybe it was the same thing; she didn't know.

Edward turned to her section boss, almost wringing his hands in delight. "One of the issues we've always had is the comptroller's concerns regarding the accounting of the inventory," he said. "So I want these two guys, who are specialists in this field," he said, with an expansive arm thrown toward the two men, "to go through our inventory processing and to look at our inventory database to see if everything is up to snuff."

Her section boss struggled to keep his jaw closed as he muttered, "I didn't think there were any problems with the inventory," he said.

"No, but I'm certain you are aware that new regulations are coming out on how medications are stored and accounted for," he said. "I want to start now because, as soon as that directive comes through, we're meant to be in compliance within thirty days."

"Normally we get months and months, if not years, for compliance," her boss muttered, frowning.

"Usually that's true," Edward said. "In this case, it's not. So I want to get a jump on it now."

Her boss sat back and frowned.

Edward nodded. "You don't like the fact that I've done this?" he asked. "You should be happy I involved you in the process."

Her boss's face immediately cleared, but she could see the effort it required of him. "I just, well, if I'm not doing a good job," he said, "it would be nice to know."

"Oh my," Edward said. "Where would you get that idea?

This is all about compliance and making sure that our processes are okay. I could have brought in a process engineer, but I thought maybe we wanted to do something much more low-key."

She slid a glance at the two men, who looked like perfect candidates to be bouncers at a bar, and wondered just what the hell low-key was—because these men were anything but.

Chapter 2

A S SOON AS Edward finished giving his orders, she was asked to take the men back to her office and to show them exactly what they were doing. She frowned at that and said, "I don't have an office to myself, and the addition of two more people will undoubtedly disturb the other two women."

Edward looked at her in surprise, then to her boss.

James frowned and shuffled papers awkwardly on his desk and said, "Other offices are on that level, so I guess we could move you two investigators to one of those for the duration of this process." He looked from the two men to Edward. "How long is this likely to take?"

"No clue," Edward said.

The first man, Johan, spoke up. "With any luck, just one week."

Her boss nodded, seemingly a little more relaxed at that. "Well, a week would not be too bad then," he said. "We obviously want to keep the disruption down to as little as possible."

"Whatever that means," Galen, the other man, murmured. But his gaze was intense and watchful, almost as if he were recording everything going on around him.

She wasn't sure what to think of them. Both men had very fair blond hair, heartily tanned skin, and prominent cheekbones with strong noses. There was just something about them. They weren't fools, but she highly doubted they were inventory process investigators though. They looked a whole lot more like thugs, the presentable kind. Then she laughed at her own musings. As soon as her laughter crept out, she immediately gulped it back, realizing how inappropriate it was.

Smiling, she got to her feet and said, "Well, we could either move the other two women out to have the men in my office, or you can put me and the investigators in another separate area. Or, you could give these guys an office near mine, and I can work there with them as needed," she said, speaking gently.

Edward nodded. "You know what? I like that last bit best because the investigators will need privacy too," he said. He looked at her boss and said, "Make it happen, James." And, with that, the same gale-force wind that blew him in now blew him right back out again.

The two men stood at the doorway and eyed James, never giving him a chance to back down from the orders that had been given him.

James shook his head and said, "In that case, I guess we'll set you up in an office." He rose, looked at Joy, and asked, "What about the office beside yours? Is that one empty?"

"I don't know," she said. To say yes would imply that she'd gone in and checked it out, which wasn't in the scope of anybody who had just started a new job. Sure, she'd been there for maybe six weeks now, but it was hardly appropriate for her to search for empty rooms.

He sighed and said, "Come on then. I'll have to get IT to give you computers."

"We have our own laptops," Johan said, his tone calm, yet brusque.

James frowned at that. "We do have heavy security here."

"Obviously," Galen said, as if James had no clue how much security they had or what and how much these men knew about it.

It was an odd conversation, but James was obviously the loser every time he opened his mouth. She didn't want to be happy about it, but she kind of was because he hadn't taken anything she'd said seriously, and that really bothered her. How could he be so dismissive when a case of missing ketamine could be all kinds of major bad news? But now she had to fall in line as they all left James's office. She studied her boss's rigid back as he strode down the hallway. Whatever was going on was something he hadn't expected, and he was obviously not impressed by having something pulled over on him.

As far as Edward went, Joy liked him. He had made things happen, and that was good.

James took them all down the elevator to her floor, and then they walked to her corner of the building, passing many closed doors, basically a series of small rooms, one after the other.

After opening several doors, James nodded and said, "This one's got a double desk. No windows though," he said, with an airy wave of his hand, as if to say they didn't need one anyway.

"That'll be fine," Johan said.

James nodded. "Good then." He stopped, looked at the two men, and said, "You need anything else?"

"I'm sure we can get what we need from Joy," Johan said

with a nod in her direction.

She raised an eyebrow but didn't say anything.

Her boss snorted. "Good. That's perfect," he said. "The least interference in the rest of this department is best." He stopped, turned, and said, "I don't have to reiterate how private all this information is, do I?"

"Not at all," Galen said calmly. "This is what we do."

Her boss didn't look very sure about that answer, but he nodded, turned, and walked away.

The three of them stood in the hallway and watched until James turned the corner. Then the men looked at her. This time she saw real smiles.

Johan said, "Kai says hi."

Immediately she felt relief wash through her. She rushed into the small room, waiting until the men closed the door. As she went to open her mouth, one of them held up a hand, pulled something from his pocket, and proceeded to check the room for something. It took her a few minutes to realize he was looking for listening devices.

"Seriously?" she asked.

When Galen had searched the room and found nothing, he nodded and stowed away the small box in his pocket. "Absolutely."

She sagged and sat down at one of the desks. "Kai really thought this was serious?"

"Didn't you?" Johan asked.

"I did," she said. "I just didn't know how bad it potentially was."

"Exactly," Johan said. "So do you want to fill us in on what's going on?"

She snorted. "I was about to ask you that same question."

"Too bad," Galen said, "we got it in first."

She glared at him, but he just responded with a grin. She shook her head. "First, before I forget, when I signed in this morning, my computer didn't go to a log-in screen. As if I didn't sign out on Friday evening."

The guys exchanged knowing looks but didn't say anything.

Frustrated at their silence, she asked, "Do you have laptops? Are you doing anything here?"

"Oh, we'll do something," Johan said. "Kai went to Ice, and Ice went to Bruce who then included Edward."

She knew about Ice because Kai had been full of admiration for her. In fact, she'd raved constantly about Ice. Kai obviously really liked the woman. It took a lot for Kai to respect anybody. "And Ice just picked up the phone and called Bruce?" Joy asked.

"That's Ice, for you," Johan said with a big cheerful rumble. "Bruce was horrified and brought Edward in to handle this, and both, by the way, were horrified."

She sagged in place and closed her eyes briefly. "Well, I'm glad to hear that," she said. "Is there any regulation coming down the pipeline that we must be in compliance with?"

"No clue," Galen said cheerfully. "We're not concerned about what's coming down the pipeline. We are more concerned about what may have gone out of here through that pipeline."

She frowned at that, thinking about it, and then realized he meant other medications, drugs, and anything else that may have left the building. "I hadn't considered that," she said. "I was just so stunned at my boss—James, whom you just met—considering it to be some clerical error."

"Is it possible?" Johan asked.

"Well, I guess," she said, "but I'm not sure. When you think about it, I suppose it's possible."

"Not only possible," he said, "it's very probable. And is this just the tip of the iceberg? Or else, somebody has just gotten started."

"Or it's a clerical error," she said drily.

He looked at her, and even Galen stared at her steadily.

She raised both hands in frustration, wondering what those shared looks meant. "Or not," she said. "I presume you guys will find out one way or the other."

They beamed. "We certainly will," Johan said. "Now, we'll need the password to get into the network, or I guess we can just hack our way in."

She gasped. "Don't do that," she said, turning to leave. "I'll get IT to come and give you a hand."

When they looked at her, she froze.

"Isn't it better if you do it legally, at least initially?" she asked, her voice rising. The two looked at each other, shrugged, then nodded. "Good," she said. "I'll go to my desk and give him a call. I'll have him come down as soon as he can."

"And then we'll go over your databases," Johan said.

"Fine. I'll be back in a few minutes." And, with that, she turned and left.

"ALMOST LOOKS LIKE she's running away. What are you thinking?" Johan asked his partner.

Galen laughed. "Definitely running away. Of course she'd have to take her eyes off you first to run very fast."

Johan snorted. "Seriously? I think she just decided both

of us were enough to scare her."

"Not sure *scare* is the right word, but she's definitely afraid she got into something that's bigger than what she initially thought."

"Good instincts," he said. "Particularly after Ice found out through one of her cop friends that they had suspicions of some drugs being moved here. So she added some suspicions of her own. She suspects the cops will tell us to back off on the ketamine investigation."

"Yeah, but why would they pin it on this place?"

"Because somebody else contacted the cops a few months ago about missing drugs. From this very building."

"Wow," Galen said. "You didn't tell me that part."

"It just came by email as we walked in."

"So, what happened to that person?"

"Her name's Chelsea. I don't know yet. We're looking into it," Johan said in a solemn voice.

"Maybe Joy is on to something then," Galen said. "I had wondered if Ice had assigned us this project as busywork to keep us around town."

"I figured we'd check this out, and, if nothing was here, we'd go make ourselves useful helping the others on the African art thefts."

"I didn't realize when she said the two cases were close together in town that she really meant side by side. Or back to back is more accurate here."

"I know," Johan said, wandering around the small space that was their office for a week or so. "We've got this massive research facility down the block, and at the end of the block is the back end of the museum. The front of the museum opens onto one of the main city streets and has a huge cultural district area set before it. But the back end of it sure isn't very far away from us here."

"Connection?" Galen mused.

"Well, it's hard not to see the potential for a connection," Johan replied. "But that doesn't mean it's the one we're thinking of. It could be anything. And it could be nothing."

"Well, let's get to work here and see if we can come up with anything useful."

Just then came a knock on the door, and a tall skinny kid with wire frame glasses poked his head in. He wore Casual Friday attire, even on Mondays, it seemed. Johan noted his security pass affixed to his T-shirt pocket, yet the outer flap on his pocket protector hid most of his photo and his name. *Not good security measures*, Johan thought.

"Hey, I'm from IT. I heard I'm supposed to hook you two up."

"Who did that come from?" Johan was testing the kid, just to be sure.

He laughed. "I got three requests, but all were the same. Edward sent me an email. James just tagged me in the hallway, and Joy called me."

"Sounds good," Johan said. "We need access to all the inventory management systems."

He looked at him in surprise. "Is that all you need?"

"Not necessarily. What did Edward say to give us access to?"

The young man took a deep breath. "He said basically everything."

"Good enough," Johan said. "That's what we need then."

"Where are your laptops?" They pulled them out, and the IT guy quickly sat them down side by side and set them both up for access to the network. "Now you guys realize an awful lot of very sensitive information is here, correct?"

"Got it," both men said smoothly.

The IT guy hesitated, and they just looked at him with blank faces. He sighed. "I get that an investigation is going on, but I want to make sure that everything stays secure. That's my job, and, if things go off the rails, I'm the one who'll get blamed for it."

"Good point," Johan said. "A very good point."

"So what's the deal then?"

"No deal," Johan said. "If we run into any trouble, we'll give you a shout."

After that obvious dismissal, the young man hesitated, then nodded and left.

"Did you catch his name?" Galen asked.

"I don't know for sure," Johan said, "but, when he entered into the admin system, he used the name Pedro."

"Good enough," Galen said. Sitting down, he looked at the inventory management area on the screen and said, "You got any clue how to proceed?"

"Hell no," Johan said. "But I guess it's like the way we do our inventory. We go into the room and count."

"Yeah, but that's just an excuse for us to play, because our inventory is guns, ammo, grenades, and anything else in the line of toys that we might have stockpiled. Hell, we all want to do inventory back home."

"I wonder if they do it the same way at Ice's compound."

"I wonder," Galen said. "Because, man, this sucks. Paperwork is a pain in the ass."

At that, Johan burst out laughing. "Well, we need to get a handle on it. Otherwise we'll let Ice down. And we can't do that."

"Nope," Galen replied. "It's a hell of a deal between her and Bullard, isn't it? I like traveling back and forth and switching out companies for a bit."

"Don't we all love that?" he said. "Don't we all."

They both fell to searching through the database.

"Johan, doesn't everything look a little too clean and neat?" Galen asked after a few minutes.

"We haven't had much time to check it over yet," he said. "First thing I'm doing though is setting up bugs on these laptops to make sure nobody is tracking our progress through the databases."

"Yeah, good idea," Galen said.

"I've already worked my way through the internet and into the network, putting little trackers on her boss James. And Joy."

"Interesting. Why Joy?"

"As the lowest on the totem pole, she's the easiest to get blamed. She's a new hire, sitting here, with access to everything. She's pretty vulnerable."

"Good point," he said. "So are you sweet on her?"

"I'm not sweet on anybody," Johan said.

"Too bad," Galen said with a laugh. "Because, if you are sweet on her, then you should know that she's interested."

"And if I'm not sweet on her?"

"Well, then maybe I'll get sweet on her," Galen said.

Johan just stared at him.

Galen looked up, a big smile rippling across his face. "So you *are* interested?"

"No, I'm not," Johan said in exasperation. "She put out a cry for help, and we've responded. That's it."

"So you haven't noticed that she's like five feet ten inches, maybe 125 pounds, with curves in all the best places? And that long blond hair? She dresses simply but with that classy attitude, and she's got legs that never quit. What's not to like?" Galen asked.

Caught off guard, Johan said, "Absolutely nothing."

Galen laughed. "See? I figured you hadn't missed out on seeing the important parts."

"Doesn't mean I'll do anything about it though," Johan said begrudgingly.

"If you aren't, I am," Galen said. "So let me know, huh?"

Chapter 3

IT WAS ALMOST impossible for Joy to stay focused on her work. Not just because the two men were here—due to her call to Kai—but also because everybody appeared to be looking at her. Or maybe it was her imagination. It didn't matter because it still felt like eyes were on her all day long. She kept glancing around the room.

Finally one of the other women, Phyllis, called her out. "What is your problem today?" she asked. "You're so antsy."

Joy shrugged. "Just a weird feeling of being watched," she said with a frown. "I've never noticed it before today."

"It's probably because the board members are here," Doris said with a laugh. "That always gives me the creeps."

"I wouldn't know them myself," Joy said.

"I think three of them are here today. It's putting everybody on edge," Phyllis said from the other side of Joy.

Joy nodded and tried to refocus. She would have to stop turning around and looking everywhere; otherwise she'd call more attention to herself, and that was the last thing she wanted.

As she went through her databases, doing inventory and bringing up lists for the purchaser to be working on, she got a phone call. She looked at her cell phone, an unusual place for her to receive calls when at work, only to see it was from Kai. Instead of answering it, Joy hit Ignore, hoping Kai would get the message.

"Was that your new boyfriend?" Phyllis asked with a laugh.

"No new boyfriend," she murmured. "The last one was enough."

"Well, that's the idea," Phyllis said. "Your last one is supposed to be enough."

It took her a moment to get it, and she chuckled. "But that one wasn't *it*. Exactly." She shifted through the stack of paperwork on the side, looking for her next priority.

"If you ever get through all that work," Doris said, "I have more that you can help me out with too."

"Good enough," Joy said. "I'll let you know when I get to the bottom of this."

"It's so great being at the bottom of the totem pole," Phyllis said. "We get all the crap work."

Joy didn't say anything, but it was true. Still it was a job, and she was grateful to have it. She hadn't been in town for very long, so this was paying the rent, while she looked for something in her field. In the back of her mind she played around with the idea of returning to school. She liked the idea of real estate too, but it was such an up-and-down job as far as income went, so it wasn't something she could really count on.

Heavy footsteps in the hallway had all three women looking up expectantly, when a large male entered their room. Phyllis primped in front of him. Joy wondered where he found suits big enough for him. And in those flashy colors. Not that he was overweight, just taller and broader than most men. His tie clashed with his suit. His attire could give her a headache in about ten minutes. Hopefully he would be gone soon.

He looked at her idly and then turned to the other two. "I'm looking for Joy."

Joy swallowed hard. "I'm Joy," she said.

His gaze locked on hers, and he nodded. "In my office, please."

Immediately she bounced up and said, "Of course, sir." She stared at him in shock, then looked at her coworkers, who exchanged worried glances with Joy. And she followed him out. She had no clue who he was.

As he led her to the elevator without saying a word, she did her best to stay neutral and unconcerned at his side. But she had no doubt that this was major. She either had no job at the end of today—or even in the next five minutes—or it had something to do with the two men who were even now downstairs in a room close to hers.

When the elevator doors opened on the penthouse floor, he led her through to a large corner office. Now she realized that this really was a bigwig. He motioned at a chair and told her to sit. She sat.

He walked around, sat down in the big leather chair on the other side of his desk, crossed his hands in front of him and said, "I spoke with Edward."

She nodded mutely.

He studied her for a moment. "Do you even know who I am?"

Immediately she shook her head.

He cracked a smile. "I guess what I should have done first was introduce myself," he said. "I'm the one who started this company."

Her breath let out with a *whoosh*. "Oh, hi."

"My name is Barlow," he said, "and you're Joy. The latest addition to the company."

She winced at that because such an odd note was in his voice that she wasn't quite sure how to react to it.

"And apparently you may prove to be the most disruptive," he said, but no humor was in his voice.

Her shoulders sagged. "I was just doing my job."

"And that's a good thing," he said. "Yet you appear to have stirred up a hornet's nest. I've had people through my office all day, complaining."

"About me?"

"Some of it, yes," he said with a laugh. "Your boss for one."

"Oh," she said, sagging in place. "So does that mean I'm fired?"

His eyebrows shot up. "Fired for doing your job? No," he said. "Obviously you've created a disruption that we need to take a closer look at."

She nodded, but, in her mind, she wondered how James, who she didn't think was all that higher above her on the totem pole, had come to Barlow's attention. "I guess he must be really upset with me if he came to you."

"Well, you would think so, wouldn't you?" he said, tilting his fingers under his chin. "And I thought it was kind of strange too."

She stared at him in surprise. "In what way?" she asked cautiously.

"In the same way that I wouldn't have expected something like that to be brought to my attention."

"Of course not," she said. "You have managers below you who take care of things."

"And I'm not even sure what all is involved," he said, "or at least I didn't until I spoke with Edward."

She just nodded, not sure what she was supposed to say.

"I looked at your résumé and your employee file," Barlow said.

She took a slow cautious breath. "Oh," she said. "I hope nothing there upset you."

"No, not at all," he said. "You have a long and eclectic history."

She winced at that. "Originally an ER nurse but burned-out. In the last couple of jobs I was considered a troubleshooter," she said, "not a troublemaker."

He burst out laughing at that. "You were a manager for a company not too long ago and sorted out some major problems within the organization. Is that correct?"

She nodded. "But it's not like I was trained for it. I just fell into the job, found some issues, and brought them up. The company was restructured to fix some of the problems."

"Do you care to explain?"

She hesitated, then shrugged. "As long as I don't give away any secrets, we're fine," she said with a smile. Then she explained how the process that the company ran had been extremely inefficient, causing several pinch points and problems within the system.

"If what you saw helped the company, then good for you."

"Then they loaned me to another company," she said in a quiet voice.

He smiled. "Did you help them too?"

She nodded slowly. "I did."

"So then, why are you here?"

"Because all of that was in Boston," she said, "and I decided that the Texas weather might suit me better."

"Now that's understandable," he said. "So you've only been here in town a little while?"

"Three months," she said.

"And this was the only job that you could get?"

"I didn't have any business contacts locally, and I have rent to pay," she said. "So I did try to get jobs that were more closely aligned to the work that I used to do, but I don't exactly have that job title per se, just the experience."

"No, it's not like you have process engineer or something as a title, do you?" he said with a questioning glance. "Any training or certifications in that field?"

She shook her head. "No, I think I'm just observant," she said quietly.

"Well, it's obviously a good skill to have but a little hard to market."

"Exactly." By now she was relaxed enough to be curious as to why he was grilling her, but, at the same time, she didn't know what the outcome of this was supposed to be. "Am I in trouble?" she asked boldly.

"No, not at all," Barlow said. "I did want to ask you just what you were doing after I saw your application form," he said, "because we do have some issues here in the company, as you are already aware. And I was contemplating using some of your skills to help us solve some of them."

She stared at him in surprise. "Oh." She didn't know what else to say. She'd sounded like a nitwit the entire time.

"And I also took it upon myself to contact a couple of your references."

She stared at him in shock. "Normally that's done before somebody's hired."

He chuckled, the waves of his silver hair rippled smoothly along his head, but she couldn't decide if he was too smooth or just somebody who saw an opportunity and wondered how he could take advantage of it.

"You should be happy to know that your references are sorry to have lost you."

"I've had several calls, wanting me back," she said.

"That's a huge compliment," he said in surprise.

She shot him a grin. "I told them they could fly me back and forth if they wanted to keep me, or they could open up satellite offices, but I was not interested in dealing with the Boston weather on a daily basis anymore."

"Both of which are potential options," he said.

She nodded. "Yes, there were some discussions about it, but, as of yet, nobody had decided to take me up on it."

"Well, that is to our advantage then," he said smoothly. "So let me just think about this. I did want to ask you just what stuff you had dealt with before. I'm glad you told me," he said, "and glad you're not upset that I contacted your references."

"Not at all," she said. Seeing that the interview was almost at an end, she stood. "If you have any other questions, just let me know."

"And I might," he said. "It will depend on the outcome of the investigation that's getting underway."

She nodded in understanding, then walked to the door and said, "Thanks for not firing me."

"No, just forgive me for giving you a heart attack, right?" And again he shot her a bright used-car-salesman smile.

She gave a small laugh. "Exactly." And, with that, she slipped out and shut the door behind her.

She stood there for a long moment, letting her breath ease from her chest, not at all surprised when she heard him as he picked up the phone and called somebody. She couldn't hear anything about the conversation, but, as she walked down the hallway, she wondered if Barlow was speaking with Edward or maybe even her section boss, James. She had no clue how her boss would handle her being here now. Would he be awkward, or would he be resentful? Or maybe he even would hate her for this. Whichever happened, not a whole lot she could do about it now. She'd lost the right to complain once she had called Kai and asked for help.

JOHAN LOOKED AT Galen. "Any luck?"

"Not yet," he muttered. "I just took some updated training on IT stuff from Stone, not that I'm sure any of it stuck yet, but I can tell you that that guy's magic when it comes to this shit."

"He's also at the end of a phone call," Johan reminded him.

Galen looked up, surprised, then nodded. "I keep forgetting. Because we're not back in Africa, I feel disconnected from the team somehow. And I forget that we have a team here."

Johan nodded. "We do, indeed, and many of them are more into the techie stuff than we are, I think."

"I am far more comfortable out in the field with a gun, but it seems like the weapons of today favor the electronic version," Galen replied.

"I know," he said. "So far I'm not seeing any irregularities with password log-ins or the timing when accessing files," he said. "I'm just going through the basics at the moment."

"Right. It'll get a whole lot more complicated as we get further into it."

"I know," Johan muttered. "Because then we must consider who might have been working under somebody else's access. Like Joy already warned us about with her computer."

"And whoever might have put in a Trojan, so that it's sitting there for them to access when they do log in, and they can worm their way into somebody else's files under their names."

"Yeah, so we gotta check out Joy's computer for sure," Johan said, staring at the computer in frustration. "I really want to blow apart our cover and the security by going in hot, delving like we normally do."

"But we can only do that after the fact," Galen said. "We can't do it here and keep our footprints hidden."

"I know. I know. But Stone could." Hearing a phone dialing, he turned to look at Galen, who was calling somebody. Johan raised an eyebrow and asked, "Stone?"

Galen nodded. Johan grinned and went back to his work. With his phone, he sent an update to Levi, letting them know where they were, what they were doing, as well as their progress so far—which wasn't a whole lot. They were hindered by the need to hide their real intent for being here. But Stone, going under the radar, could find a whole helluva lot more. Johan could hear Galen behind him, conversing with Stone over something that Galen had found. So far Johan hadn't found much. When an internal chat window popped up, and the IT administrator, who turned out to be Pedro, asked if they needed anything, Johan wondered if something they had done had triggered that response. **I don't think so yet. Why?**

The chat window came back up. **Just checking in.**

We're doing fine.

He waited to see if the kid would come back with something else, but, when he didn't, Johan figured that the kid had been watching them, tracking them in the system. Had the kid seen what they were looking at? Or that they were in incognito mode and had lots of ways of getting in and searching for stuff? Yet Johan didn't know what kind of a hacker the kid might be, and that was always a bit of a disconcerting moment.

Just then a knock came at their door.

"Come in," Johan called out.

Joy popped her head around the door. She smiled and said, "I was wondering if you guys wanted some coffee."

He looked at her in surprise and then nodded slowly. "That would be great. Is there a coffeepot around?"

"It's on the other end," she said. "I'll go grab two cups." She stopped as she was about to exit, then turned and asked, "Black?"

"It's the only way," he said with a smile.

She grinned back and headed out.

Johan thought of Galen's earlier words as she disappeared. She really was a sweetie. Not to mention gorgeous. It would certainly complicate his life to have a relationship over here. If it was short with no strings, that was one thing; but, if it got to be serious, well, that would stop him from going back to Africa, at least right away.

Maybe that was okay too. He shrugged it off as he delved a little further, wondering exactly what he was seeing.

When she returned a few minutes later, she carried three cups of coffee.

He immediately stood and took two from her hands, as she attempted to set them on his desk.

"I'm not very clumsy normally," she said, "but these are big mugs." She shrugged and added, "I figured, if I was making the trip, I might as well get a cup for myself too."

They were also quite hot. Johan distributed one cup to Galen, who still talked quietly on the phone with Stone, while working on his laptop. Because Galen was talking, Johan didn't want to disturb his partner, so he motioned to the doorway and asked Joy, "Can anybody hear us out there?"

"Possibly," she said. "I don't know what's in the other rooms." She looked over at Galen, then frowned and asked, "Who is he talking to about our system?"

Johan just gave a shrug, not committing to anything.

She eyed him carefully and then said, "I'm not supposed to know, am I?"

"It's better if you don't," he said gently.

She sighed and nodded. "I wanted to tell you about a strange meeting I just got called up to."

His eyebrows shot up, and he pulled her back into the room and closed the door. He sat her down in the chair beside him and asked in a low voice, "What happened?"

She told him about the visit with Barlow, who was the original creator of the company.

"Now that's interesting," Johan said slowly. "Obviously the upper echelon of the company is hearing about us being here."

"Barlow said he talked to Edward," she stated, by way of explanation. "And also that my section boss, James, had talked to Barlow about what I had found."

"Well, that's good, I would think," he said quietly, cautiously.

"Yes," she said with half a smile. "A hierarchy's in place, and we go up from one level to the next to the next, like I did by going to James first."

Johan chuckled. "I don't think anything is quite so normal here anymore," he said. "When it looks like a shake-down will be happening, people start jumping as high as they can to save themselves."

"I get that," she said. "Barlow did ask me about my previous jobs and the work I did, but I didn't quite understand where he was coming from."

"Keep an eye out," he said, "because it's hard to say."

"Right."

He stopped, looked at her, and asked, "Did you consider the fact that maybe he was offering you a better job?"

She gave him a wry look. "If that's what he was doing," she said, "I'm just wondering ..." And she hesitated.

He looked at her seriously. "If you have any doubts, or if your instincts are telling you that it's something other than what it appears to be on the surface, then tell me," he said. "We can't deal with a threat if we don't understand how dangerous it is."

"He was friendly and all," she said slowly, "but I did wonder if maybe he wasn't dangling something in front of me."

"And, if he was," Johan said, "was it a reward or a bribe?"

"That's what I was afraid of," she said, her voice dropping to barely above a whisper. "Because I don't want to deal with that."

"The previous company you worked for, did you have any trouble with them?"

"No, none," she said. "Once we realized I had a talent for it, I went in to help other companies relieve the pinch points in their processing, or whatever it was they were doing. And you know what? All three companies I worked with alleviated some major kinks in their systems. But, when

I got here, I needed a job to pay the rent, and so this is what I ended up applying for because I couldn't land a job that I preferred."

"Yeah, process engineering is not exactly an easily marketable skill," he said, "but then maybe a recruiter could have helped you with that."

"I was pretty unconcerned about it at the time. I was just delighted to be away from the Boston winters and was enjoying traveling around and being part of Texas," she said. "Eventually reality set in, and I needed a job because the rent had to be paid. This job offered me an opportunity to do that, so I accepted the position."

"So you took it while you could look around for something better," he said, noting her wry expression at his words.

She nodded. "Let's hope James and Edward and Barlow didn't figure that out too," she said.

He laughed. "Doesn't matter if they did or not. Corporations all over know their prize employees are prime targets for headhunters. You try to keep the good employees. You obviously have skills, and you are smart enough to do what you need to do," he said. "So whatever they figure out doesn't really matter."

"That's true enough," she said, "but I still have that pesky rent to pay."

He grinned. "Yep, I hear you."

She stood and said, "I need to get back to work too."

"Well, if anybody says anything about you being here," he said, "just tell him—or her—that I needed information."

"And you did," she said with a smile as she left.

He watched her go, only to hear Galen beside him. "What was that all about?"

He turned to look at his buddy and quickly explained

what she just told him.

"Interesting," Galen said. "Definitely suspicious."

"Yet innocent enough on the surface. Smart even because, if she has a skill that they could use, of course they would want to bring along someone they've already got on board and make better use of those skills." He looked at Galen's laptop. "Did Stone help?"

"Absolutely," he said.

"Good. I might have to give him a call a little later too."

"I saw how you were looking at her, by the way," Galen said, a smile in his voice.

Johan shot his friend a disgusted look. "She's pretty, so how else can I look at her?"

"No way. I saw *that* look," Galen said smugly. "Which is a whole lot more than just about her being pretty."

"Well, in that case," Johan said, "*that* is your answer."

Galen looked confused for a moment. "To what question?"

"As to whether I'm interested or not," he said. "So now she is off-limits for you."

Immediately Galen's face fell.

But Johan just laughed out loud, delighted with himself.

Chapter 4

THE REST OF the week was a repeat of Monday. She came into work, buckled down to the stacks of paper she had to go through, got up with her clipboard to double-check various things that needed checking, and wandered past the men working in the next room, and, most of the time, found them there. When they weren't there, she stopped and wondered where the hell they were. But nobody talked to her about it. She had no more strange meetings. No more strange *anything* really, just the sense of being part of a conspiracy against the company. And that felt wrong too. Her section boss never called her upstairs anymore, and the other two women just kept working at her side. Nobody made any comments about anything.

On Friday, Johan stopped at her doorway and asked to speak with her for a few minutes. Surprised, she stood and walked toward him. "Is there something I can help you with?"

He motioned her out into the hallway and said in a low voice, "Come out for lunch with us."

She checked her watch and nodded. "I have lunch with me today," she said, "but I guess I can have it for dinner tonight. My lunch break is in about five minutes."

"We'll wait in the parking lot for you," he murmured before he turned and walked away.

She headed back in to find the two women staring at her. She just shrugged and didn't say anything. She sat back down to her work, but she only had a couple more minutes before she left again. One of the ladies, Doris, got up to go, leaving just Phyllis here.

"You got something going with that hunky investigator?" Phyllis asked.

Surprised, Joy looked at her and blushed. "No," she said. "I don't."

"Well, you should," she said. "You definitely should. He's perfect. Real dream material and he's interested."

"Maybe so," Joy said, "but that doesn't mean he's available."

"Who cares?" Phyllis said carelessly. "Have a night's romp and enjoy it. If he's got a wife back home, it's not like you'll be hurting her."

Joy hated that attitude but kept the smile pinned to her face. It never did any good to make enemies in the office.

Phyllis stood and stretched, then said, "I've got another half hour before I go to lunch," she said, "but I have to take a pee break." With that, she rushed from the office.

Joy wasn't sure if Phyllis really was going to the ladies' room or not, but, regardless, it was Joy's lunchtime now. So, logging off her computer, she grabbed her purse, slung it over her shoulder, and walked to the nearest exit. She didn't pass anybody on the way, but, for days now, she had felt like she was being watched.

Outside, she walked to the large parking lot, unsure where the guys were. A truck pulled up, and, seeing Galen in the passenger seat, Joy hopped into the back, and they quickly drove away.

"Will anybody see me in here?" she asked, leaning forward.

"Won't matter. We'll change the vehicle after lunch," Galen said.

"You realize that, since you guys showed up, it feels like I'm being watched all the time?"

Johan, who was driving, caught her gaze in the rearview mirror. "Seriously?"

"Yes. At first, I kept turning around, and the women finally snapped at me because I was bugging them. But it just feels wrong."

"And it's from behind you in your office?"

She nodded. "And, yeah, I did look but didn't see any cameras or anything terribly obvious."

"Interesting," they murmured.

"Other than that, it's been really quiet," she said. "Almost too quiet."

"In what way?"

"Normally I would have meetings with my section boss once a day, or every couple days at least, just touching base to see what's happening with my work, that type of thing. James has avoided me entirely this week."

"Well, today's Friday, so it will be interesting to see what he's like next week."

"I don't know," she said. "Something just feels wrong."

"Good point," Johan said. "We'll be doing some work in the office over the weekend."

"They're letting you in?"

"Well, we do have a pretty high security clearance," he said, "but we'll be doing a lot of it through remote access."

"That makes more sense," she said. "Did you guys have a reason for bringing me outside the office for lunch?"

"We would wait until the end of the day," he said, "but

we figured we'd start now."

Not liking the mysterious way they'd explained it, she said, "Well, I hope I get lunch at the same time."

They burst out laughing. "We'll go to a restaurant up ahead," Johan said, pulling into a restaurant parking lot.

They hopped out. It was one of those casual café places and kind of noisy. She was surprised; obviously they wouldn't be talking about anything to do with work in this place.

They quickly ordered lunch, paid for it, and headed for a table at a far corner, where it was quieter, carrying a little wooden card with a number on it. They placed it on the table so the server could find them when their order was ready.

She glanced around and said, "I don't know this place."

"Not a surprise if you haven't had much time to get out yet," Johan said.

"Since I started working, there hasn't been any time at all."

"What do you do when you go home?" Johan asked casually.

"Laundry and cooking," she said promptly. "Grocery shopping too because I never seem to get enough at once, and I'm still trying to find stores that carry some of my favorite foods. By the time I get home, I'm usually too tired for much else."

They nodded, and a long silence ensued.

Finally she couldn't stand it any longer. "Did you guys find anything?" she whispered.

"Yep," they both said.

"But it goes deep," came the response from Galen.

She sagged in her chair. "I was so hoping that you

wouldn't find anything, that it was all just a clerical error."

"But you also knew it wasn't," Johan said, "and that's why you contacted Kai."

"Yeah. I should call her. I think I'm due for a girls' night out." She reached up to rub her temples. "Will I have to look for a new job?"

"It wouldn't be a bad idea," Galen said. "Not too sure how the company will rebound after all this becomes public."

"It'll become public?" she asked in horror. "They hire an awful lot of people. I'd hate to think they could all lose their jobs over this."

"Well, what we don't know at the moment," Johan said, "is how many people are involved."

She turned up her nose at that. "Over 240 staff work there," she said, "so I can't imagine that very many have anything to do with the issue we're dealing with."

"No, but we'll probably find one in every department," he said. "How else do you hide office theft otherwise?"

She thought about it and shrugged. "I don't know. Maybe someone just in accounting and somebody who had physical access to nick the drugs."

"What about the purchaser who brings it in?" Johan threw it out there for her to think about. "What if the research lab is bringing in way more than they need and charging Westgroup for it, and then only so much is showing up on the shelves?"

"That's possible, but then I wouldn't have seen it noted as inventory, and, in that case, it wouldn't have gone missing," she said slowly. "So, that doesn't make a whole lot of sense or—" and she stopped.

Both men looked at her and nodded in approval. "Or?"

Johan prodded.

"Or," she said, "more than one person is involved."

"Not only more than one person is involved," he said, "but more than one person is trying to steal the drugs, from the things we've found so far."

She stared at him. "How high is the rate of employee theft in something like this globally?" she asked curiously.

"Globally?" Galen turned to look at Johan. "Not sure about globally but I'd say it's pretty damn high. Probably ten percent."

"Ten percent of companies have internal theft problems?"

"Not all companies suffer from employee theft," Johan added. "I'm sure *all* the drug companies have a much higher incidence of that crime, due to the money to be made on the black market. And the percentage of internal theft is much higher too when you're talking about medications, drugs, or any addictive substances like this. Now, if you're just talking about office supplies, many people don't even consider that theft. Tons of people take stuff home. Pads of paper, printer paper, notebooks, diaries, planners, and lots of other office supplies—like, you know, just pens stuck in their pockets or purses absentmindedly—and not necessarily with the intent to steal but to work at home, even though they haven't signed it out or whatever."

"Yes, I've seen a lot of that too," she murmured. "Even things like, you know, packages of coffee disappear far too quickly."

"With that kind of office supply stuff, the incidence of employee theft is extremely high, yet the cost to replace those items is nothing compared to replacing drugs. But picking up a whole case of ketamine? That is something entirely different."

"Right," she said, "and it makes absolutely no sense to me."

"What do you know about a woman named Chelsea?" Johan asked.

"Don't even know the name," she said promptly.

"Interesting," he said.

She studied Johan for a long moment. "Obviously it's important, but I don't know who she is or why you're bringing her up."

"She had your job before you did."

"I don't remember them saying I was replacing some-body. I thought they said they had split the job duties and now needed a new person." She found herself trying to think back to exactly what happened. Then she shrugged. "I don't remember what they said," she confessed. "Is it important?"

"Not necessarily," he said. "We do know that she used to work at the company, and she held your position."

"So, whatever I was told was a lie?"

"Or potentially a job reshuffling did happen, and the title was changed," Galen suggested.

"That's possible too. So, what about this Chelsea?" She looked from one man to the other, waiting to hear more.

Galen nodded to Johan, who spoke up. "Well, that's one of the things we wanted to know, if you'd heard anything about her from anybody."

"Honestly, no. Nobody has mentioned her at all," she said. "Now you're worrying me as to why not."

"Well, she's dead for one thing."

As bombshells went, that was a big one. Any reaction by Joy was cut off just then, as the waitress arrived with large plates of food. She put burgers and fries down in front of the guys and a big salad in front of her. Joy looked at it, then looked at theirs. "Dang, yours looks better than mine."

Johan immediately offered her some of his.

"No. The salad's better for me." But she reached across to snag a fry off his plate. "I will take this though."

He smiled and said, "Plenty more if you want them."

She nodded and dug into her salad, while she tried to figure out who this Chelsea person was. "I work with two women. We've done some talking, not much," she said. "They don't seem to like each other, and they both really don't like me. But so far neither has mentioned a Chelsea."

"And, if you were to bring her up now," Johan said, "it would be suspicious."

"Very," she said. "I'm not sure how I can find anything out."

"Well, we've been into her employee file, and we've certainly checked what she was doing within the computer system, but there doesn't appear to be anything suspicious, outside of the fact that she's dead."

"How did she die?"

"A hit-and-run," Johan said.

Joy sank back in her chair. "Murdered, you think?" she asked, looking around to see if anybody heard her.

"Well, vehicular, as in manslaughter, is probably the charge that would be brought if the cops ever found out who did it," Galen said. "But, according to the police, they don't have a lead."

She stared at her salad, suddenly not hungry. "Is there any reason to think it was deliberate?"

Both men shook their heads. Johan added, "Not at the moment."

She let out her pent-up breath. "Well, that's something

at least," she murmured.

"It is," Johan said, "but we're a little worried and want to make sure you stay safe."

"Is there anything in her history that shows she raised the alarm over any other missing stuff?"

"No. Nothing we've found so far," Johan replied. "Yet files can be deleted, altered, or made into what they weren't."

"What about her friends and family? Can you talk to them?"

"She was new to town, and her apartment has already been leased. Her mother didn't have anything to offer and didn't want to talk much about her daughter."

"Can't you find any of Chelsea's friends, at work or elsewhere?"

"The cops already have," Galen said, "and we have a copy of their file on Chelsea, but we don't have anything to go on yet."

Knowing she needed the food, even though her stomach was now churning uneasily, she finished her salad and put the plate off to the side, pulling her large mug of coffee toward her. "That's a little unsettling," she announced.

"We're not telling you to upset you," Johan said. "We're telling you so you stay aware."

She gave him a flat stare. "Aware of what? Being run down in the dark? Aware of an intruder? Aware that somebody may want to target me? What are you saying?"

"All of the above," Galen said.

She just stared at him in shock.

Johan nodded. "What you may have just opened up is one huge can of worms," he said. "It could be that it's not just centered within this company, and it could have been operating for a very long time, considering that Westgroup has been in operation for forty-odd years. Just think about how many drugs could have potentially gone missing if there was cooperation within the company?"

"That's all a little raw to think about," she said slowly.

"It's more than that," Galen said. "It's dangerous as hell. We don't have any connection from Chelsea's death to the company, but we don't want to find a connection too late and take any chances by not giving you a heads-up."

Her breath let out with a heavy *whoosh*. "And I live alone, so thanks for that. Now I won't sleep again," she snapped, looking from one to the other.

"Better you sleep aware and wake up versus not being aware of the dangers and risk never waking up," Johan said.

The waitress came and took away Joy's plate. Joy watched as the woman strode off toward the kitchen, Joy's mind already on a million other things. It was the mundane reality of the everyday world that often helped Joy to reset her mind. "Sounds like a pattern is here," she muttered.

The men looked at her. "In what way?"

"It's hard to say," she said, "but one of the things that I do like, or seem to find, are processes. Whether it's a process within the company, and that's a good process, or it's a process that, in this case, is not good. I think a process is working inside the company's processes," she said. "I know that sounds confusing as hell, but someone somewhere along that line has a pinch point," she said, crossing her arms over her chest, and she leaned back against the chair. "And I intend to find it."

JOHAN KNEW A bit about what she had mentioned with pinch points and internal corporate processes from a previous job or two he had done. But those were dealing with chemical pinch points or mechanical pinch points, where physical problems could occur with employees. She was talking about theoretical pinch points or software pinch points here, like a double set of books or cooking the online books.

Even though the cops had been cooperative in sharing with Johan and Galen what little they had in Chelsea's investigation file, the police had confirmed what Ice had said earlier. The detective was very clear and told Johan to back off the missing ketamine case and any attempts into delving further into Chelsea's death. Those were his cases.

Still, like Ice had informed Harrison about the art theft case, Ice also instructed Johan that he and Galen would continue with their investigations into all elements as needed. That easily took care of that.

However, Johan didn't know if Joy had taken the possible threat against her life seriously or not, given Chelsea's fate, but everything inside Johan said that, instead of making her wary or more alert, the crime had fascinated her and had made her more determined to get to the bottom of it. And somebody who followed software processes to figure out where the pinch points were must have an interesting turn of mind. The fact that she was even intrigued by it fascinated him. Galen was right; something was very unusual about her. And Johan wanted to know more.

After they dropped her off again at the front entrance to the building, Johan drove around to the far side of the parking lot and parked. He hopped out, and Galen switched over to the driver's side.

"I'll be back with a different vehicle in an hour," Galen said.

"Right. I'll head back to the books," Johan said.

He wasn't really looking at the books, of course, but at the network, the security access for each employee, and the timing throughout the day when files were accessed and things like that.

When he came to the States to temporarily stay at Levi's compound, Johan hadn't really expected to be doing cyberwork. But he should have because that was a lot of what Levi did. As Johan walked down the hall toward his assigned space near the back exit, he passed a couple people who completely ignored him. Of course that had been the way of it since he'd arrived. He and Galen were strangers. Nobody knew anything about them, but nobody seemed to care one way or the other. And that was good with Johan. Being a shadow in the hallway gave him all kinds of access.

Just as the men were about to walk out the exit, Johan turned to catch sight of one of them turning to look at him. Johan smiled when the other man hurriedly turned away.

"Nice to meet you too," he muttered to himself, as he meandered his way through the building, checking out what was behind various doors. Mostly storerooms were down here and several underground truck accesses, per the blueprints he had seen. He needed to make his way down there to the docks at some point and the lower levels as well.

He paused, thought about it, and, when he came to an exit with stairs going down, he decided it was the perfect time. He slipped through and headed all the way down, noting the cameras on various landings. Only in this one, there wasn't any at the door he had come through. So far, people could come and go easily.

He'd have to check the hallway to see what cameras focused on that door. And he needed to find out how long they held the video feeds. Some places didn't have the space to store endless security feeds and ditched them after twenty-four hours, which was completely useless in Johan's mind.

As far as he was concerned, thirty days was a minimum. Particularly given the high-tech level of what this theft could have been. That also bothered him. Missing a physical case of drugs like that was a very low-tech theft, as if somebody made a quick decision, grabbed it, and ran.

He couldn't put that thought out of his mind either. It's quite possible that Chelsea, the woman Joy replaced, could have done just that, but why? Johan knew nothing about her really. She had been here for three months before she died. *No, that doesn't track,* Johan thought. *If she had come here to work with Westgroup, intent on stealing drugs, she'd have done it her first week here and then disappeared, before all her employee data was proved to be fabricated. Unless she had somehow been embraced by the thieves. Nah, doesn't make sense either to accept a newbie within a long-term crew. More likely she had found an inventory problem, like Joy had, and had mentioned it to the wrong people.*

Johan continued to ponder it further as he headed down yet another set of stairs. There had been one landing above, but, when he'd seen the other stairs, he couldn't resist. He was now two stories below where he had been. It ended here, so he opened the double doors and stepped out.

He checked the darkened hallway, but he found no signs to direct him down here. And this level wasn't the actual research lab; that was down the block. This may have been where some of the online research was done behind locked doors, he presumed, but not with animals. He sure hadn't seen any here.

He wandered all the way down on that level, going to

every door that he couldn't access, only to find his key card didn't let him into very much at all. He'd been told he'd have full access but apparently not down here.

And, of course, every time his card was swiped, it should have shown up on the security feed. So, if somebody was watching what he was doing, they would know exactly where he was. If this were his company, he'd make damn sure that every time somebody's security card didn't work in an unauthorized area, somebody armed and in uniform would be checking, in person, to see where the offenders were. Johan could only hope that was the case here. Yet he had already been at this for a good fifteen minutes, and no one was chasing him down. Johan shook his head. Still, he'd also been given clearance at the highest level, and he could go where he wanted without question.

He wandered down a little farther and found several more locked doors that didn't have security card readers. He checked to see if any cameras were in this area but didn't find any. That concerned him too. He snorted. "It's a wonder they aren't missing a ton more drugs."

He had his wallet out and his tiny pick in hand a moment later. He'd learned a lot of skills on the job, and making sure he was never stuck without a way to get in and to get out of places was one of them. He had the lock picked and the door open in thirteen seconds flat.

By the time he slipped in and turned on the light, he could see he was in yet another storeroom full of boxes. He just didn't know what they were full of.

He wandered through, looking at shipping labels, trying to tell what the boxes held. He quickly took photos and sent them to Levi. But, interestingly enough, nothing that he did allowed the photos to send. The icon on his phone just kept spinning. Studying the concrete walls, he noted he was too deep underground and the walls were too thick to allow the signals to go through.

He wandered through the boxes before taking out his pocketknife and cutting one of them open. It appeared to be medical supplies, but nothing he opened revealed any drugs. Just cotton swabs and tongue depressors and medical tape mostly. Why were medical supplies here? Was this just an overflow area for the real lab down the block? Like a place to store stuff they couldn't take all at once? But why would you do that? That's a recipe to lose things. Plus, if all this was for the big lab down the street, how the hell did they do inventory if stuff was left here? Johan shook his head. "Not a profitable way to do business."

The shipping docks weren't here, so somebody would have to hand truck all this stuff here from the bays and leave it. Then hand truck it all back out to retrieve it to possibly transport it to the lab. Granted the truckers making the deliveries couldn't know what was inside these boxes any more than Johan could tell, not without opening them up. Yet the random labels Johan had checked were all for this building. Why?

Frowning, he stepped out of this storeroom, with as much intel as he could get from that room in one efficient visit, then went through the next room and did the same thing. Again he found more stuff, but this stash was separated into different groupings. One area appeared to be office stuff. Another had old newspapers, cages, feeders, and that type of thing for animals. Shaking his head, he went through the whole room, spot-checking and taking pictures again, then headed to the third and last locked room on this level. He wondered what the hell was going on here, and what kind of a crazy filing system they had for all the random stuff stuck down here.

He bet that Joy knew nothing about all this and that her records wouldn't entail any of it as well. *What was going on here?* As he stepped through the door into the last room, he froze because it sounded like somebody was inside. Then he noted a flashlight beam. So Johan didn't turn on the overhead light and immediately dropped to the ground and crept onto the other side behind the doorway. He waited and listened. He was a pro at this. Whoever was in here had to be aware that he'd entered, and now they would be worried about what he was up to.

He smiled at that, because when it came to playing a game of cat and mouse, Johan was definitely the cat. He heard a semiscuffle, as if somebody was to his right and was sliding closer to the doorway. *Amateur.* Silently Johan shifted across to the boxes in front of him, keeping out of sight, but leaving the pathway open for whoever it was who wanted to escape.

He heard another movement and another, as Johan slid a little bit closer. What the stranger didn't know, possibly because of the angle of the doorway and how it entered the small hallway, was whether Johan had come in or whether he just opened the door and then left. Now Johan could hear his heavy labored breathing, panicked and moist.

Johan let his eyes adjust to the darkness, hoping to see a shape, a shadow, something. With the next movement, an outline took form. Male, five feet, eight inches, maybe 160 pounds. Casually dressed. The stranger took another step forward. Johan pondered his options. He could give himself away by catching the stranger now, or he could see who this person was and do a check on him before approaching him later. Then the man raced to the door in a sudden panic and opened it.

He disappeared into the darkness.

Maybe because he didn't want to get caught in the act of stealing? Johan thought. *Or maybe because he had just stumbled onto this too? If he's one of the good guys, he could have run because he might have thought I was one of the bad guys.*

Johan stayed where he was and immediately noted the impressions of what he'd seen on his phone, hoping to match this guy's description with a name soon. He'd check all the photos in the personnel files. Then he stood, turned on the light, and checked out the room. This room was a different matter entirely. This was completely full of medications. All with labels for Westgroup. Johan took several photos of multiple cases, and, when he was done, he stepped out into the hallway, took a photo of the hallway with these doors.

There was one more hallway around the corner, which he took. It led to more stairs. As he walked up the stairs, it took him directly to the loading docks. Johan looked back, wondering if he'd missed an elevator somewhere. Because it would make more sense to go from the loading dock with all these cases of inventory via an elevator to these storage rooms on another level.

He retraced his steps and, sure enough, against the wall in the half-darkness was an elevator. He immediately looked for a control panel, but it was flush against the wall. Johan was surprised when he got it opened with no security card needed at all and stepped inside, checking out what the options were inside the car. What he saw caused him to whistle. Because that elevator led right to the top floor. No other choices were given. All the way to the penthouse and the corner offices of this building.

He quickly took a photo of the two elevator stops, designated simply as *P* and *B3*, and stepped back out again. Then he went up the stairs and stepped out into the loading dock bays. Several men unloaded a bunch of materials, as several others, and what looked like a trucker, stood there, talking. Johan quickly scanned the men, looking for the stranger he had crossed paths with in that last storeroom. He sighed when nobody matched up.

At his sudden presence, they all turned and stared at him. He gave a half smile and didn't make any explanations as he walked over to the truck and studied the interior.

"Hey, who are you and what are you doing here?"

Just enough anger was in his voice that Johan immediately spun around to look at him.

One of the bigger of the six men came toward him.

"Just checking out what you're doing," he said, noting this guy had a Westgroup employee photo ID badge. Yet his workers did not. So Westgroup had hired the foreman, probably letting him dole out the work to independent contractors, field laborers even. Did Westgroup have enough trucking needs to have a full-time foreman on hand? Maybe the foreman was part-time. More questions. "I'm part of a two-man team of investigators here, looking into some specific issues," he said calmly. He deliberately kept his voice mild as he waited to hear what the other man would say.

The foreman took a step back, his hands on his hips. He wore one of those yellow safety vests, with his employee card dangling from a lanyard on top. Grabbing the front edges of the vest, he glared. "Well, your investigation doesn't have anything to do with anything down here."

"How do you know?" Johan asked in a mild tone. He studied the other men, who were all collecting around the first man. Nobody but the foreman wore a name tag, so Johan carefully took a moment to study their faces so he'd remember them later.

"We haven't been told about anything," said one of the men in the back.

"Do the higher-ups talk to you about things going on in the company all the time?" Johan asked with genuine curiosity.

Finding out how a company worked was just as important as how it wasn't working. For all Johan knew, everybody was involved in this scam from top to bottom. And yet he still hadn't found any proof of any internal scam, so maybe it was his mind-set that automatically determined everybody was guilty until proven innocent.

"If it's major, yes," the foreman said, "so you need to get the hell out of here."

"And why is that?" Johan asked, not moving.

"Well, for one thing," one of the guys said, "you don't have safety boots on." A couple guys around him grinned because that was generally a safe bet.

"Quite right, I don't," he said. "But no machinery's operating at the moment." Turning to look at the truck, he asked, "What are you unloading?"

"Boxes," the foreman in front sneered. "And, if you don't get out of here, we'll call our manager down here."

Johan spun around and said, "Please do."

That stopped the foreman flat-footed. He looked at the others and frowned.

"Are you really doing an investigation?" asked one of the men in the back. It was the same one who had mocked

Johan over the lack of safety boots.

Johan nodded slowly. "Yes, I really am," he said.

"About what?"

"Something that affects every level of the company," he said. "Obviously I'm not at liberty to give you too many details."

"Well, you can give us one," the foreman snapped.

"Theft and smuggling. There's two." He said it more to see their reaction, hoping they would react in a way that would help him somehow.

At that, several of the men's faces turned bleach-white, which Johan noted with interest, but the foreman in the front just turned bubbly red. "Well, you sure as hell don't need to be rooting around accusing us," he roared.

"Did I say I was?"

"You're down here," he snapped. "That's all the evidence I need."

"Interesting," he said. "So the fact that I'm down here checking things out bothers you? So far, I haven't seen anything, but, at the moment, it looks like you guys are trying to interfere with my job."

That set the men back a little as well.

Johan waved a hand at them. "Carry on with your jobs," he said. "I'm just here to observe."

They frowned and shuffled their feet, but the man in charge nodded at them and motioned at the truck. "Get moving," he said. "We haven't got all day. We've got two more trucks coming in."

"How do you move the material from here to the research center?"

"We don't." The guy looked at Johan in surprise. "Why would we? That would defeat the purpose. If they're on a truck already, you might as well just truck them over there."

"That's what I was thinking," Johan said in a mild tone.

The guy stared at him in confusion.

Johan just smiled and stepped out of the way when the men returned to the truck to unload the rest of the boxes. Because he was watching, of course, they went about it in a fast and efficient manner, trying to look good. And he could appreciate that.

While they did their thing, Johan wandered around and studied the view, the access, the cameras, and security. The guy who was obviously in charge walked over and said, "If you've got any questions, ask me please, and don't disturb the guys."

"I'll ask whoever I want to ask," Johan said, without even turning around. He knew that would insult almost everybody and wanted to see what would set off these guys. Were they company men, or would they be upset at their employer and be ready to haul ass out of here?

He could hear the snort from the guy behind him, but Johan continued to walk, looking at the equipment and noting everything was well maintained, parked nicely and neatly out of the way, and that safety was obviously a prime concern. He nodded approvingly.

"What?" asked the foreman.

Johan looked at him. "Don't be so touchy," he said. "I was just noticing how clean and well maintained everything is and how safety appears to be paramount."

"It is," he said proudly. "We haven't had an accident down here in over four years."

"And considering you're running a lot of forklifts," Johan said, "that's impressive."

"Injuries happen regardless of the forklifts," he said.

"You get guys who lift boxes improperly, guys who load up crap and don't watch where they're going, or don't wear their safety gear," he said with a shake of his head. "I got no use for that."

Johan nodded in an understanding way.

The foreman relaxed. "It's hard to keep track of all these guys, you know?" he said confidentially. "They come and they go, and you think you got them broken of their bad habits because you watch over them like a hawk."

"That's because the bosses never understand how easy it is for accidents to happen. They just look at you and say, 'Why the hell didn't you stop it?' Right?"

The foreman reached up and rubbed a little bit of white fluff remaining on the top of his almost bare head. "Isn't that the truth," he muttered. "The last guy dropped a box on his foot and broke his toe. Somehow I was supposed to stop that. They forgot about the fact that he lifted the box properly, carried it properly, and checked his pathway carefully."

"Right. Dropping a box is pretty darn easy," Johan said. "Surely somebody in management gets that."

"Whatever was inside the box caused the chaos," he said. "I don't even know what it was, but it was damn heavy, and everything's supposed to be packed under fifty pounds for personal lifting," he said. "If we'd realized it was heavier, we would have used equipment. But it's never that simple. Part of doing our job means we have to rely on other people to do theirs."

At that, Johan laughed. "I think that's a complaint the whole world over."

"It is, indeed," he said.

With the other man obviously easing his outrage, Johan

nodded. "Looks like you've got this well in hand."

"Well, I do," he said, "but I only work five days a week."

"Right. So you're full-time, I presume."

The foreman nodded.

"So is this area open the other two days?"

"We don't have any receiving coming in those two days," he said. "But, of course, the lab guys are moving stuff up and down as needed."

"Are the offices all closed on the weekends?"

"From what I know, yes. Not the lab," he said. "They have to check up on stuff all the time, so that stays pretty busy on weekends."

"Makes sense," Johan said. "I'll find out for sure, as I'll be in tomorrow too."

The other guy looked at him in surprise, then shrugged and said, "Makes sense," he said. "At least you'll have access to what you need then."

"That's the plan," Johan said. He took a step back, smiled at the foreman, and said, "I'll leave you to your work then." Johan turned, catching the relief spread over the man's face as Johan headed back out to the loading bay, where he jumped down to the concrete slab and walked out to where he could turn and look at where the bays were situated on the actual building.

The bay doors were flush with the wall, and some windows were up above, but the lights didn't appear to be on, or the rooms weren't occupied at present, at least from what Johan could tell. He knew the other men were standing and watching him as he headed backward, looking at the entire layout of the building and the property itself. But Johan had to check not just the microstuff but also the macro as well.

When he got to the edge of the parking lot, almost to

the driveway out onto the main road, he turned to look at all the buildings around. It was a heavy commercial-industrial area here. At least on this side and heading off in one direction. Yet the backside of the museum could be seen from here, but that building fronted another road, more or less marking off the arts district of downtown Houston.

Everybody on this side, fronting the nearest road, had big trucks, huge driveways, and wire fences between the places, all with gates that could be locked up at nighttime and weeds that seemed to be heavier all along the fence line.

The problem with that was it was pretty easy to hide a cut or to bend a portion of the fence to gain access—even how somebody dug down beneath the fence in order to get under it. Something that he'd have to take note of. He pulled out his phone and deliberately took several photos of the fence line and then of the building itself, as he walked around to the front so he could go in through the reception area. He checked out the parking lot that he passed on his way. The loading docks were in the back, with a parking lot on this side, a parking lot on the far side, and then in the front was the visitor parking.

Finished with his external inspection, Johan walked back inside the front reception area. The woman at the front desk looked up at him in surprise and asked, "May I help you, sir?"

He lifted his pass, smiled, and walked right past her through the security doors behind her.

She called out, "Sorry, can I—" and, with that, he was gone.

He wasn't sure if she would call somebody or come after him herself. But, when she didn't come through the connecting door, he figured that was his answer. *Security around here sucks.*

At the first set of stairs, he headed back down to his office. Once he got there, he noted that Galen still hadn't returned. He checked his watch, frowned, and sent him a text. **You coming back anytime soon?**

On my way. Just passed you outside.

Yeah. Been looking at the loading bays, the various basement levels, and access to all. Found three doors locked with no security, all full of boxes of products. One guy was in the third, which was full of drugs.

Interesting. That was all Galen said.

Yeah. Uploading a bunch of material for Levi to look at.

Johan sat down at his laptop, went to his email, and quickly checked if anybody had been through his system. It was clean. With that, he sent Levi a zip folder with all the pictures he'd taken with his phone and the notes he'd taken, including everything about the random inventory in the three locked rooms and a description of the stranger. He included a note.

Levi, zip file with pics attached. Not sure what any of this is or if it's important, but wonder what the deal is with three locked doors without the typical keypad security or cameras. Odd collection stored. One guy hiding in the shadows in the third one that held drugs.

Then he hit Send. By the time he got through the other emails that had downloaded into his mailbox, he looked up to see Galen walking in with two coffees. Johan smiled. "You know what? I keep thinking there's got to be a place around pretty close where we can grab good coffee, and then I forget when I'm out."

"Got you covered," Galen said and set one down on the desk in front of him. "So tell me what you found."

Johan hopped up, walked over to close the door, then explained what he'd seen, occasionally referencing his photos. They brought up a blueprint to the building on his laptop. He looked at it and frowned. "*Hmm.* Not seeing the rooms I was in today."

"Added afterward, you think?"

"That would make sense," he said, "especially if you really don't want people to know."

"So then, were they done on purpose for this stealing event, or was somebody just taking advantage of empty space? I mean, they probably figured that because those rooms weren't on the blueprint or that people didn't know about them, they were safe enough for their purposes?"

"Lots of questions. Again, just no answers."

"What was the loading bay like?" Galen asked.

"The usual stuff. You know? 'Get out of my turf. This is my space. We're fine without you. Take your investigation somewhere else.' All the usual crap."

Galen laughed. "Turf wars are normal. If you were to go to the front receptionist and say you were doing an investigation, she'd be the same way."

"Yeah. I just flashed my card at her and kept going and thought she was gonna chase me down as it was," Johan said cheerfully.

Then he showed Galen the photos he had taken from the inside the locked rooms.

"Very interesting," Galen said. "But why? A lot of material is here. Seems like wasted money, right?"

"The question is, has it just been forgotten? Because it's just stuck down there and who cares? Or is it something people are moving in and out secretly? Or is this something that accidentally got dumped here because they didn't have storage space at the big lab, or maybe they needed to move it somewhere else. Like an unusual or unexpected event. Remember though. The lab itself is down the block, but we still have some researchers in this building. However, I think they are more online researchers, not actual researchers testing formulas in a lab. So I don't see how our in-house researchers would need the medicines and the medical supplies and such. Do you?"

Galen shook his head. "Who would know the differences between any research guys here and those at the lab itself? Much less any physical inventory designated for the online research guys here and the actual lab guys down the block?"

"Potentially the foreman from the shipping dock, who's a full-time employee by the way."

"Interesting," Galen responded.

"Potentially anybody dealing with inventory."

"Like Joy?"

"Or the one before her."

"We can't ask Chelsea anymore," Galen said, "but what if she found this stockpile of undocumented inventory?"

"I don't know," Johan said, sitting back at his desk, reaching for his coffee. He flipped the plastic lid off the top and took a sip. "But, if any of this material has been purchased, it's got to be going through the corporate accounts, right?"

"I haven't seen anything like this so far in the books, though it's early."

"Right, so I'm wondering whether somebody doesn't have a fake account that all this material is running in and out of, so nobody's the wiser."

"And the point of the fake account would be like to launder money, only this is to launder inventory. Is that what you're saying?" Galen asked.

"Exactly."

"So then," Galen continued, "money in, money out, but where are they siphoning the money in from and where would the money go out to?"

"Well, possibly it's the company's money to begin with, that they're just shuffling around. Think three-card monte, just the online version," Johan mused. "It's also possible that they're moving this for somebody else, a third party."

"That almost makes more sense too," Galen said, "and there'll be a million excuses as to why they can't take possession of the shipment right now."

Johan thought about that and then nodded. "And that brings up a lot of other options too, doesn't it?"

Galen looked at him, gave a wry smile, and said, "Absolutely."

Chapter 5

JOY WATCHED AS Johan walked past her office, but he wasn't even looking in her direction.

"You really are stuck on him, aren't you?" Phyllis said, from beside her.

She looked at her coworker, surprised. "Why do you say that?"

"Every time you hear footsteps, you look up."

"You don't?" she challenged.

"Nope, I sure don't," Phyllis said. "Nobody I care about here."

"A lot of people are here," Joy said. "Surely you could find somebody as a potential partner."

"Not interested," she said. "Working together kills a relationship."

"Are you even after a relationship?" Joy asked. "Sounds like a roll in the hay is what you're after."

"Whatever. Either way, it's still bad news."

A note in her voice made Joy wonder if Phyllis hadn't already tried it and had paid the price for the indiscretion. Considering where she worked, maybe so. "Good point," she said. "I don't think it's a good idea myself either." She noted the empty chair beside them. "Is Doris coming back today?"

Phyllis looked up, gave a shrug, and said, "Who knows?"

Something about Phyllis and her complete detachment

to everything except for whatever Joy was doing made her feel slightly uncomfortable. And unnerved.

Finally Phyllis got up and said, "I have to get out of here." And she left the room.

Fascinated, Joy watched as her coworker walked away. Phyllis didn't say she would go to the washroom or to get a coffee from the lunchroom, just that she *needed to get out of here*. But then the scenario for Joy was different. She already knew the chances of her staying here long-term were pretty small. And she certainly wouldn't work in this small windowless hovel of an office very long. Yet, while she didn't understand what the processes were in this company, she wanted to.

She didn't know if her visit with the owner had been more of a nudge to her subconscious, throwing her a potential bone down the road more than anything. But she'd already started mapping out how the processes in the company worked. Little snippets of information available from lots of different people were starting to give bits of insight into how things were managed and how the company worked. She'd enjoyed lunch with the guys and wished she had the ability to talk openly with the men. It would make being here a lot easier.

When more footsteps headed down the hallway, she looked up, catching sight of somebody she didn't expect to see. *Edward.* But he walked past her office to visit with the two men next door. When she heard raised voices, she frowned, wondering if she should join them.

When Phyllis came racing back in, her expression was a picture of delight. She said, "Oh, my God, they're all fighting!"

"Who?" Joy asked.

"The investigators and Edward."

"That's bizarre," Joy said. "Why Edward?"

"I don't know. I don't know," Phyllis said, dancing with joy. "I need another excuse to go out."

"Fine. Go get me coffee," Joy said.

Phyllis nodded, grabbed her cup, and left. The second she was gone, Joy got up and walked over to the wall that separated them from the office next door and tried to listen.

"You shouldn't have gone in there," Edward raged.

"And why is that?" Johan asked.

"The foreman came to me to find out what the hell was going on."

"And do you know what's going on?" he asked.

"Yes, Ice told me, but we have to be discreet. You told them you were investigating theft and smuggling. That's hardly being discreet."

"They're honest workers who would appreciate an honest answer," he said. "Obviously everybody'll be wondering what we're doing down here in the dungeon."

"Let them wonder," Edward said. "I don't want any more leaks getting out."

"It got out the minute you brought us in," Johan said. "I've had stares from everyone."

Then an odd silence prevailed, as if both men had reduced the volume of their voices.

Frowning and disappointed, Joy quickly slipped back to her desk to resume her work. She shoved a piece of paper under her laptop that she had prepared, showing the processes as she collected information. Just then, Phyllis came back in with her coffee. "Looks like they've stopped fighting," she said with disappointment. "And they've also shut the door."

"I imagine somebody in the company is not too happy about the investigators being here," Joy said.

"Hell, who would be?" Phyllis said. "Think about it. Everybody becomes a suspect." She looked at Joy. "Even you."

"I haven't been here long enough to get into trouble," she said, knowing that was a lie. Because that's exactly what she'd done. She'd gotten into trouble immediately. Dangerously so, apparently. It was frustrating as heck too.

"Oh, I don't know about that," Phyllis said. "Chelsea wasn't here very long, and she was the one before you."

That was the first Joy had ever heard mention of anybody *before* her. "So somebody was in this job before me?" she asked curiously. "I wondered because there doesn't seem to be anything really in place."

"Chelsea was at that desk, but she didn't last longer than three months."

"Oh, so that's a warning for me then," Joy said with an eye roll.

"Yeah. I think two people before her, the higher-ups combined the position and changed job duties or something," Phyllis said with a wave of her hand. "Useless management stuff that they keep pulling on us."

"Isn't that the truth?" Joy said. "I hope Chelsea found a better job."

"I presume so. She was here and then gone," Phyllis said. "I never did hear what happened to her."

At that, Joy froze and turned to look at her. "Didn't you even ask?"

"Nope. She knew her three-month probationary period was up on that Friday, and she herself was wondering if she wanted to stay or not," she said. "I just figured she didn't. I mean, you've seen this place. Can you blame her?"

"Don't you have to give notice?"

"We're supposed to," Phyllis said, "but who knows. Maybe it was worth it to them to let her quit and just leave. That way they didn't have to let her go."

"Why would they let her go? That's a little depressing," she said.

"It is what it is. You can't count on it one day to the next. Deal with it and do the best you can for yourself," Phyllis said. "All places are shit to work for."

"Now that's depressing too," she said, with a laughing smile.

"But it's the truth, unless you're working for yourself and are making money at it. We're all just selling our time to somebody, and it doesn't matter who anymore. So pick somebody you can live with and go from there," she said.

It was an interesting attitude, but then, as Joy had discovered, Phyllis had an interesting attitude on a lot of things. "Sounds very much like it's a case of *look after yourself and forget the rest.*"

Phyllis sat back and gave her a stern look. "And you remember that," she said, "because, just when you think the world is going your way, somebody will come along, cut you off at the knees, and stick you in a place like this." She sneered, as she looked around the windowless office. "I used to have a big corner office here," she said. "I was somebody then, and now I'm nobody."

Joy winced at that. "Wow," she said, "I'm sorry."

"Whatever. It happened so long ago, I don't even know if very many people remember anymore."

"How long ago?" she asked impulsively. She couldn't imagine going from the top to the bottom, yet still being at the same company.

"It was twenty-four years ago," she said with a note of bitterness.

"And you stayed?"

"I left for a while, about five years, but that didn't work out so well. I tried a few other jobs and then figured that I'd just take something down here and get a paycheck," she said.

"I'm surprised they hired you back," Joy said, not meaning to insult her. "I mean, just think about it. You know? If people still remembered you ..."

"The only one who still remembers me is Barlow," she said. "I think everybody else is new."

"Edward too?"

"Edward is wet behind the ears," she said.

"I'm sorry though," Joy said. "It's got to be tough."

"It was very tough," she said. "And then I grew thicker skin."

And that was the end of it as far as Phyllis was concerned. But given the rest that Joy knew was going on here, she wondered if it was that easy. Was Phyllis the kind of person who would just ignore what was happening around her? Maybe so, Joy suspected, but it was almost like Phyllis was insulated from everything. She didn't give a shit, didn't care; she just did her job, took a weekly paycheck, and left. There were worse things to do, if she had something else in her life. However, from the sounds of it, all she really had were one-night stands with whatever guys she picked up here and there. And that was starting to give the impression of a very sad life.

With curiosity pushing at her to keep asking questions, Joy was tempted to continue, but she didn't want to piss off Phyllis. Reluctantly Joy put her head down to work, feeling an awkward silence between them.

Finally Phyllis laughed out loud. "Your curiosity is almost palpable. Do you know that?"

Joy sat back and released a frustrated sigh. "And I was trying to be so good."

"I slept with him, okay? I slept with him." Shaking her head, Phyllis went on. "I thought we were a team. We'd been together for years, after all." She shook her head again with a sigh. "And then he screwed me over."

But no bitterness was in her voice, no rancor. That's what amazed Joy. "Yet you seem to have gotten over it," she said.

"No, not really," she said. "The breakup was brutal, and I got demoted. He accused me of all kinds of nastiness, including stealing secrets from the company," she said with a snort. "What the hell would I do with those?" she demanded. "I had hoped the two of us would get married and have a family." She rubbed her temples. "But it's all water under the bridge now."

"I guess I just don't understand why you're still here," Joy said tentatively. She honestly didn't understand. If it had been her, this was the last place she'd want to be. "I sure wouldn't ever want to see him again, much less at my job," she muttered. "I'd go out of my way to avoid him for sure."

"And I did for a while," Phyllis said with a shrug. "But now there's almost a certain satisfaction in knowing that he's still single and that he doesn't have a proper relationship. I'm well past it and just want to sit on the sidelines and watch the show."

"No bitterness?"

"Nah, not now," she said with a laugh. "It's a big joke. The joke's on me, but I'm okay with it now. Back then? Oh, hell no," she said. "I was definitely a woman scorned. That's one of the reasons I left. But, when I couldn't find another job or a company I was comfortable with, I came back. Five years later was just enough time for people to have forgotten, plus I looked different. I'd gained about twenty-five pounds, was older, and worked in a completely different department."

"But your name?"

"Yeah, my name is the same," she said. "But back then, I was called by my nickname all the time, *Philly*. Now I just go by Phyllis."

"I'm sorry. That's still a tough one."

"Which is why I said, if you're going to sleep with somebody, take what you want and run, because they won't be there for you tomorrow."

"I hate to think it's the same for everybody," Joy said. "I haven't ever been married, but I'd still like to believe in it."

"Maybe," she said. "At least legally you'd get something out of the deal. I got nothing."

"Sorry again," she muttered.

Phyllis shrugged and went back to her work, but Joy found it hard to concentrate. She tried to associate Phyllis's words with Barlow, the man she'd met in his office. He did have that smarmy snake-oil front, but what would he have been like twenty-four years ago? And why would he have dumped Phyllis like that? That's not normal behavior either.

But then nothing seemed to be normal about this. Joy wasn't great on human behavior because she had always been an optimist, looking for the better side of people. But too often that came back and bit her in the ass. Still, it was better than being like them.

When her phone rang with a call, she picked it up to

hear Kai on the other end.

"Hey, sweetie," Kai said. "How about dinner?"

"Are you coming into town?"

"Yep, I'll be there by five."

"I'd love to go for dinner then," she said. "Just the two of us?"

"Nope, not that easy," Kai said. "The guys will be joining us."

"Perfect," she said, "and what about your beau?"

"He's coming too," Kai said. "We're both on jobs so often that any chance we can be together, we take advantage of that."

"At five o'clock then?"

"Perfect," Kai said, "and we'll probably have a varied evening, so don't dress up."

She hung up after that, leaving Joy staring at her phone, wondering what *a varied evening* meant. She shook her head and had just gotten back to work when Phyllis said, "When you go out on that date, remember what I told you," she said. "Take what you can because he's won't be there for you tomorrow."

"Got it," she muttered. The thing was, Kai had been there for Joy a lot already. She already knew the woman inside and out. And Kai was gold—the real deal. Joy was just sorry that Phyllis hadn't had anybody in her life she could count on.

AT THE END of the workday Johan stepped out the front door to Westgroup and took several deep breaths of fresh air. He'd been going through so many lines of code that his brain needed to be cleared. Levi had also gotten hold of them, saying they'd found irregularities with four different accounts. Apparently Levi had somebody at the compound who loved to do forensic accounting. Johan couldn't believe it because that was an insane way to spend your day. Although he would love to talk to her when he got back.

Galen stepped up beside him. "You ready?"

"Yeah. I'm ready for anything but more code," he said.

Galen laughed. "We're too much of the shoot-him-up kind of fighters," he said. "All this cyberstuff seems cowardly and manipulative."

"Which is what people have been doing to each other since the beginning of time," he said.

Just then the door opened again, and Joy stepped out. She looked at the men with surprise. "Hey," she said. "You guys okay?"

"Any reason we wouldn't be?" Johan asked.

She smiled. "I heard all the hollering over there earlier."

Johan laughed. "Yeah, Edward wasn't too pleased with my visit to the shipping dock."

"Whatever," she said. "But he's the one who helped bring you in."

"True enough." They walked toward the parking lot.

"Are you guys coming for dinner tonight?"

They nodded.

She frowned, looking at her watch. "We don't have a whole lot of time."

"We'll follow you back to your place," they said.

She nodded, slipped into her small car, and they pulled up behind her. They were now driving an SUV, as anonymous as anything else on the road.

"Nobody has checked her place yet, have they?" Galen asked from the driver's seat.

"No. I took a couple looks in her office today, but I couldn't see any cameras. We need to get a bug detector in there."

"Kai is bringing some today," Galen said.

"Good. We'll check it over this weekend," Johan replied. They had a full weekend planned, so tonight's dinner would be a little bit of a break before they got downright serious.

"Do we have anything to give them?"

"Lots of suppositions and problems," he said. "There is definitely an issue at the company. What I can't figure out is how far back it goes."

"I hear you."

Galen pulled in behind her in the front of the apartment building, as she hopped out of her car. She walked around to them. "I'll just get changed."

"Good," Johan said. "I'll come up with you."

She frowned at him. "You don't have to."

"Doesn't matter if I have to or not," he said gently. "I'm coming."

She rolled her eyes at him and looked at Galen. "Are you staying here?"

"I am," he said with a grin. "So don't be long, you two."

She gave him a startled look, then glanced hesitantly at Johan and bolted to the front door of her building. Johan just looked at his partner and sighed. "You got to make it more difficult for me?"

"It's always better to have something you need to fight for," Galen said.

"Bullshit," Johan said in response.

Galen just laughed at him.

Johan quickly picked up the pace and followed behind her. She held the front door open for him, and he slipped into the hallway with her.

"What is Galen laughing at?" she asked hesitantly.

"Just a joke he made."

"About me?"

"You're a beautiful woman," Johan said. "We're both single guys. I'm sure your mind has no trouble connecting the dots."

She didn't look like she knew if she should be pleased or insulted over that. She just shrugged, and he appreciated her leaving it alone. She stepped into the elevator, and he followed.

"You're on the third floor, correct?"

She nodded. "Yes."

Seconds later the elevator door closed, and it moved upward.

"How long have you lived here?"

"Two months roughly," she said. "I stayed with some friends for a bit and then a hotel. Afterward I grabbed this apartment."

He nodded. "How's the security?"

"It's only okay," she said. "Nothing high-end about this place. I'm also on a month-to-month, so there's really no incentive for the landlord or the owners to increase the security. Or improve anything else, for that matter."

"Understood," he said.

As they walked down the hallway, she pulled out her key, unlocked the door, and stepped inside. He followed. It was small, maybe eight hundred square feet. A one-bedroom apartment where the kitchen, dining room, and living room were together, with the bedroom off to the side and the bathroom opposite.

"Like I said, nothing fancy." She tossed down her purse.

"Excuse me." She walked into the bathroom first and then through to her bedroom.

Immediately he crossed the living room and pulled back the drapes to look outside, finding a small Juliet balcony. So he opened the glass doors and stepped out onto it. He could access the neighbors' balconies from hers, but it would take a bit of finagling to make it happen. He looked up to see a fourth-floor balcony directly above him. And another one down below. Pretty standard. An unassuming, nonthreatening, but easily accessed apartment. None of it made him feel any better. He stepped back inside, locked the glass doors, and closed the curtains again.

Joy came out, wearing leggings and a long lightweight tunic. He looked at her approvingly. "Kai said not to dress up," she said with a frown.

"Good," he said.

"Do you know where we're going?"

"Haven't a clue," he said. "Does it matter?"

She shrugged. "No. Yet I don't want to be overdressed or underdressed."

"How about you just go as you are and forget the status quo?" he said.

"Well, that's what I'm trying to do," she said, laughing. She walked back over, picked up her purse, and said, "You ready?"

"I am," he said, and he walked out, watching as she locked the door. "Let's take the stairs."

"Fine," she said. "But why?"

"I want to see if there's any security or cameras here," he said. "There aren't any on your floor, and I didn't see anything in the elevator."

"I didn't even look," she confessed.

He'd come to expect that sort of thing. "You don't until a predator is around," he said. "Then it's too late to wish you'd changed things."

"Well, changing things here won't be easy," she said. "If somebody comes in, there's not a whole lot I can do about it."

"Hence our concern," he said cheerfully, as they walked down the stairs.

And, indeed, no security cameras of any kind were in the stairwell either. As they walked outside, they headed back to Galen, who still sat in the SUV.

"Maybe I should drive myself," she said.

"No," Johan said. "We'll meet them there." He opened the front passenger door for her.

She hopped in and said, "I don't want to take your seat."

He just sighed and closed the door gently, then popped into the back.

"I'm not being difficult," she announced.

He burst out laughing. "No, of course not."

She subsided into what appeared to be a bit of a temper fit, and he was happy to see it. So far she'd been far too amiable, considering all that was going on.

"If you're going to be mean," she said, "I won't tell you what I found out."

"Well, you'll definitely tell us then," he said, leaning forward. "What was it?"

She launched into an explanation of what Phyllis had said about her odd relationship with Barlow and the company. Both men were dumbstruck.

"So she goes from being at the top of the company immediately down to the bottom?" Johan recapped. "And comes back after five years to spend—what? The next nineteen years in the basement? Sounds like she's punishing herself for her stupidity, but, man, she should be well over it by now."

"Yes, my thoughts too," Joy agreed. "Phyllis said she and Barlow had had a relationship for years, but I don't know what 'years' means."

"Right? Like was it really years, like three or whatever, or was it just her saying that," Johan asked.

"Do you believe her story?" Galen asked.

"I'm not sure," she said. "It was an odd thing, even for Phyllis."

"Yes, I can see that," he said.

"Not too many people would tolerate that situation either," Johan noted.

"Well, her attitude is very much about her now. I don't know if she would have had anything to do with this missing ketamine though," she said.

"It's hard to say, but you're right," Galen said. "It is an odd thing."

"Thanks for telling us." Johan settled back. He pulled out his phone, wrote down a few more notes, and sent a message to Levi, asking him to check on Phyllis and the owner.

"And I wonder if he's had any relationships since?" Galen asked.

"She said all were unsuccessful."

"In the twenty-four years since he broke up with Phyllis though, there has to be a bunch," Johan said from the back seat. "So we need to find out who they were."

"Do you think they'll have anything to do with this?" she asked in astonishment, twisting in her seat to look at him.

"No, I can't say that," he said. "But again what we want to do is make sure we check out every avenue."

"Got it," she said. "I was trying to figure out the processes of the company, but there really isn't anything I've found so far," she said. "The lab and the research side are all separated from the corporate side, at least on the books. Everything that's done in my building is more of the business, marketing, and accounting side, with a small online research group somewhere within our building too. There's no manufacturing. At least none that I have any access to. It's all at the big lab facility."

"So where did all the extra supplies come from in those lower basement areas?"

"What extra supplies? What basement levels?" she asked. When both men stared at her in surprise, she shook her head.

Johan explained about the three locked rooms on B3 that didn't show up on the blueprints.

"I had no idea." She frowned, deeply concerned. "How am I supposed to do my job if I don't know about this?"

"Maybe that's the point," Galen said.

"What does that mean?" Joy asked testily.

Johan explained, "That you're not supposed to know, so you can't interfere with their plans."

Joy's eyes went wide, but she didn't voice her fears.

Johan admired her courage. She needed to hear about all they had discovered, so she would be properly informed. "I spoke to the foreman in charge of the loading docks. They bring in truckloads of boxes that are unloaded in the shipping bays, and then his workers distribute everything to where it needs to be, basically those three locked rooms I found."

"But there shouldn't be very much here in the way of chemicals and medicines, right?" Galen asked.

"According to my records, just for the big lab down the block," she said. "All the trials and heavy-duty dangerous chemical-manufacturing stuff are done at the main lab's research center."

"Interesting. And I wonder what else happens there?" Galen asked.

"I don't know," she said. "Not sure I want to either."

He nodded. "Particularly if it involves animals."

"So, should there really be that much stuff coming and going then from your building?" Johan asked her.

"That depends what you mean by 'that much stuff,' I suppose," she said. "I don't deal with a ton of the shipping. That would be more for our purchasing officer and the accountant to reconcile between themselves."

"And yet a truck was unloading, a big truck. Unloading boxes with three forklifts down there."

She twisted around in her seat to stare at him. "Three forklifts? Why would they need so many supplies?"

"I don't know," he said. "That's what I'm trying to figure out. What exactly are they unloading here, and do people realize what's coming in and what's going out?"

Joy shook her head, her eyes wide.

"It's also possible," Galen said, "that you're dealing with one company, but the building is shared by another company, and the one company owns it."

"Meaning, the one I work for is an umbrella company?"

"Exactly. They could be dealing with some shipping import-export company on the other side or something."

"Well, that makes sense," she said, "particularly if it's related to their research."

"Maybe we need to look at that more deeply," Johan said. "It should have already been mentioned though, if that were the case."

"I don't think anybody here volunteers any information," Galen said. "They're all stuck on sticking to themselves, heads in the sand, ignoring whatever is going on there."

"Unfortunately that's very true," she said. "I was really surprised when Phyllis went off on her tirade today and explained all that about her relationship with Barlow."

"And that in itself is unusual, correct?"

"Well, I've shared an office with her for six weeks now, and she's been barely civil," she said. "But she's barely civil to Doris too. So I think the argument today that you guys had with Edward set her off."

"Interesting."

"Very."

Johan sat back, thinking about what they didn't know, and wrote down more notes to send to Levi. "We still don't have an awful lot of information," he said. "It would sure be helpful to get someone to open up to us."

"But is that cooperation necessary for you to investigate anyway?" she asked.

"Maybe not," he said. "Either we find out the information now, or we must find it later. Personally I'd rather get the information now, so I have what I need to know before I head into any dangerous situations."

"What is dangerous though?" Joy asked. "If there is a secondary company working within the same building, then it easily could have been just a mix-up in inventory."

"So, in that case, why didn't somebody just tell you or us about the second company?"

"I don't know," she said, pulling up her phone. "I almost want to call James and ask him."

"I wouldn't," he said. "It's too dangerous. You don't know what else is going on out there. James could be just a middleman."

"But 240 people work for this company," she said. "So it doesn't sound like there's room in this building for more than that. Granted, a bunch of the employees on file could be those who work at the main lab research facility down the block. I've never really done an employee canvass."

"But, if it's an umbrella company, maybe they work for someone else?" Galen offered.

"Lots of people think they work for one company," Johan said, "but legally, on paper, they're working for somebody else."

"I guess," she said. "It's kind of sad though that I've been there for six weeks, and I still haven't figured out any of this." She settled into her passenger seat, again facing forward. "But back to Phyllis. I sure wouldn't want to be in her shoes."

"No. I can't imagine that she's taken the whole thing very easily."

"And yet I want to find her guilty of something, but she hasn't stolen anything that we know of, and I think that's wrong too," she murmured. "Surely James is guilty of something, right?"

Galen laughed. "You're beginning to sound like us."

"We'll find out who's behind all this," Johan said.

"If there even is any *this*," she muttered. "So far it's just one case of ketamine missing. Although Phyllis did mention Chelsea today."

"Good! What did she say?"

Joy quickly relayed the little bit that she'd heard. And then said, "But that's really not definitive either."

Just then Galen pulled into a parking lot of a park. Johan unbuckled his seat belt, hopped out, and opened her door. She looked up at him in surprise, but he was busy searching the area.

"So, are you trying to be gallant?" she whispered in a low voice, as she stepped to the ground and leaned toward him. "Or are you thinking of my safety?"

He looked down at her, his gaze warming as he studied her worried face. "Does it bother you either way? Regardless of those two choices, I mean."

"Well, I don't know if I'm supposed to be worried about my safety too," she said. "I never really had anybody be this attentive."

"Well, maybe it's a good thing I'm here then," he said. He swooped a hand up, lifting her chin gently, and he kissed her on her nose.

She gasped and frowned. "What was that for?"

"Because I wanted to," he said with a smile.

She gave him a good frown. "Well, don't do it again."

He chuckled. "Why not?"

"Because I didn't give you permission," she said.

"Do I need permission to kiss you?" he asked with interest.

She looked immediately flustered. "Well, yes. So don't do that."

Immediately he leaned down and kissed her on the nose again. "I didn't ask for permission that time. Does that mean it's a problem?"

She glared up at him, shoving her chin toward him and asked, "What are you up to?"

He grinned, wrapping his arms around her, pulling her close, and whispered, "Maybe anything and everything I can possibly get up to," he said. "What would you say to that?"

She stared up at him, confusion clouding her gaze, and, in spite of everything going on, he reached up his hand, sliding into her curls and against her scalp. Then, holding her head in place, he lowered his lips and kissed her. When he finally broke away from her, her gaze was softly muted and completely unfocused. "Maybe I should do that again," he whispered against her lips.

"And maybe you shouldn't," she said, struggling to right herself.

He chuckled, then leaned forward and gave her a gentle peck on the lips. "Too late."

Chapter 6

JOY WAS FLUMMOXED and completely confused as to what Johan was up to. She managed to deflect the jokes from Galen, but, as they walked to a large outdoor park, she stopped and frowned. "Are we meeting Kai here?"

Just then came a call from the other side of the park. Screaming at the top of her lungs, Kai yelled, "Joy! Over here!"

Looking that way, she saw her friend, standing with her partner, Tyson. Joy raised a hand and started walking quickly toward them. Galen and Johan walked on either side of her. She glanced from one to the other.

"Why out here?" she muttered.

"Because it's a beautiful day," Johan said.

She snorted. "I still need dinner," she announced, her voice slightly contrary. But then she blamed Johan for that. Just as she was about to run the last few feet toward Kai, Johan reached out his hand and gently slipped it through her elbow, slowing her pace. She looked at him and glared. "Why?"

"For appearances," he said smoothly.

"I'm running toward a friend," she said in exasperation. "Do you guys really think we were followed here?"

"If anybody cares about what you are up to, then, yes," Galen said from the other side of her.

She frowned. "And what difference does it make if I walk or run these last few feet?"

"Maybe nothing," Johan said. "But this way, if anybody is watching, they'll know you're not alone."

She shrugged. "That doesn't make any sense."

He let his hand drop now, since they were only a couple yards away, and Kai was running toward Joy now. Kai threw open her arms, and the two women hugged.

Joy held Kai close. "Seems like it's been so long," Joy said.

Kai just chuckled. "And it's only been a couple weeks," she said, "but we've been in a drought. You were in Boston for long enough that we only saw each other every couple of years. Now that you're this close, I'm not sure what it'll take to feel like you're close enough."

"I know what you mean," Joy said. She walked over and held out her hand to Tyson.

But Tyson smiled quietly—then wrapped her up in a big hug. She appreciated it and squeezed him right back. She really liked Tyson, though she hadn't had a ton of time to get to know him. But he was one of those quiet indomitable presences behind the very small, very outgoing dynamo that was Kai, but a man completely self-contained and knowledgeable in his own right. As she stepped free, she snagged Kai into a second hug. "And why are we meeting here?" she exclaimed. "Why not a restaurant or at least my place?"

"Because we haven't swept your place yet," Tyson said, "and a restaurant has a lot of people."

"So we're out in the middle of a park? Doesn't that mean people are out here too?"

"There's the potential for a lot of people," Johan said, "but it doesn't mean they will be within earshot of us here."

She shot him a look and stepped a few feet away from him and caught Kai's knowing glance. She winced at that.

One of Kai's eyebrows shot up as she glanced between Joy and Johan, and a half smile formed.

Joy glared at her friend. "No," she stated.

Kai's grin widened, but she nodded. "If you say so," she murmured.

Joy turned to look and saw the three men standing together, talking.

Kai immediately stepped closer. "So what's going on between the two of you?"

"Nothing," Joy snapped.

"Well, obviously not nothing," Kai said with a big grin.

Knowing there was no way she could explain away or dissuade her friend from her current train of thought, Joy tried to change the conversation. "So what is really going on here? Why are we meeting in a park?"

"After hearing that your predecessor at work was killed in a hit-and-run," Kai said worriedly, "I want to convince you to leave the company."

Immediately Joy frowned. "Leaving is one thing, but leaving right now is another."

"Leaving right now would be best," Kai argued. "It would keep you safe."

Joy turned her gaze to the sky. How could she explain how she felt to Kai? Up above was a bright blue sky dotted with white clouds that moved swiftly across, as if propelled by the winds. Maybe that's how she felt too. "I feel like I need to stay and to figure out what happened."

"It's obviously dangerous," Kai said. "We don't want anything to happen to you."

"Neither do I," Joy said. "But, once that investigation

opened up, all it did was make things more dangerous for me."

"Exactly," Kai said. "And we don't want that. Yet we do need to figure out what's going on."

"But it's too late now to shield me," Joy said gently, "short of me leaving the city, which I really don't want to do. Even if I leave the company and stay here in Houston, they would know where I live, and they could still run me down. Even if I do move, that could happen regardless."

"We can protect you," Kai said instantly.

Joy stared down at her friend and smiled. "I get that you believe you can," she said, "but honestly it won't be that easy. I'm not letting you chain me to my apartment, and I don't want to have a chaperone every time I go out. So, in truth, you can't protect me all the time, and, if somebody really wanted to come after me, you know they'd find a way. The same as you would, if that were your job."

"Possibly," Kai said with a slight nod. "But you could stay safer. At work, you're a sitting duck."

"At work," she said, "I'm under Galen's and Johan's watchful eyes and hardly in any danger there."

Kai just stared at her in growing frustration.

Joy reached out to her worried friend, stole a quick hug, and said, "I'm fine. But I'm not one to walk away from trouble."

"I wish you would," Kai said. "You don't even have any self-defense knowledge."

"I have a little," she said, "but, no, nothing like you." She turned, looked around at the picnic table, then walked over, hopped up, so she sat on the tabletop with her feet on the bench. "Are we planning on eating? I don't know about anybody else, but I'm really hungry," she complained.

"We ate lunch," Johan said. "Did you not get enough?"

"I had enough lunch to get me to dinner," she said. "But now it's dinnertime, and I'm really hungry."

At that, Kai laughed. "We have food in the vehicle," she said. "Come on. Let's go get it."

"So it's a picnic then?" Joy asked.

"To a certain extent, yes," Kai said. "It's a nice sunny day out, but did you want to go somewhere else instead?"

Immediately feeling guilty, Joy knew it was rude to be so churlish, especially since they had obviously made these plans. "Oh, no, it's fine," she said. "If I want something afterward, I can always go get a coffee."

"We all can," Tyson said, and he nodded toward Kai. "Stay here and visit. I'll get the baskets."

She nodded brightly, watching him as he strode away.

"You look like you're still really happy with him," Joy said.

"I am," she whispered, and she held up her hand, proudly displaying an engagement ring.

Joy stared at it in shock and then squealed as she wrapped her arms around her friend. "Oh, Kai, I'm so happy for you," she said.

"I am too," Kai said. "It seems like now that Levi and Ice are married, the engagements are popping up all over the place."

"I'm not surprised," Joy said. "I've learned enough about them from you to see how everybody was waiting for them to get there first."

"We're not having a big wedding," she said. "In fact, we might even slip off in the dark of night and get married, then come back and have it all over with," Kai said.

"And yet maybe those you work with wouldn't appreciate that. What about those who work with Tyson?"

"I think they all would understand," she said with a laugh. "My company is doing really well, but my employees' focus is definitely not on the same stage of life as mine."

"Well, I'm glad to hear your company is doing well," she said. "There's got to be some good things in life."

"There are lots of good things," she said firmly. "Just bad circumstances resulted in you ending up in a difficult place."

"Maybe," she said. "But, now that I'm here, it's pretty hard to get out of it."

"I hear you," Kai said, "but we're here to help."

"Is it a habit that you automatically launch a full-blown investigation when a friend calls for help?"

Laughing, the two women discussed Kai's wedding plans, as Johan and Galen walked over to the table to join them. Soon Tyson was in sight, carrying two large picnic baskets. The guys grinned.

"Alfred and Bailey by any chance?" Johan asked.

"Absolutely, and we picked up coffee on the way," Tyson said. "If you guys will grab these, I'll go get the coffee."

Johan snatched one out of his hand and Galen reached for the other. They returned, placing the baskets on the picnic table.

JOHAN LOOKED DOWN at the heavy baskets. "How many people were you planning on feeding?" he joked with Kai.

"Well, I know for a fact that Joy can eat a lot," she said in a teasing manner. "And, with you guys around, there's never enough food."

Johan took things out of the baskets, and Kai walked

around the wooden picnic table and helped. Plates, cutlery, and cups were included. Then Johan brought out a dish wrapped in a heatproof bag. He pulled the dish free, and the fresh aroma of a warm bacon and spinach quiche filled the air. Also homemade buns had been wrapped up in towels, with sliced roast beef and cheese to go with them.

Joy sat down with a huge smile. "I can't believe how lucky you are to get fed like this all the time," she said.

By that time they had everything unloaded, including not only a fruit salad but a big Caesar salad to go with it all as well. After they had it all served up on plates before them, still some was left for seconds. Johan nodded in appreciation.

Joy immediately got to work on her quiche. "Gosh," she murmured around a mouthful, "it's perfect."

"It is good, isn't it?" Johan said and picked up his piece and ate it like pizza. He noted two quiches were here, which was great because Joy was already through her first serving.

He watched as she ate, loving the appetite she had and the enjoyment so evident as she devoured her food. She had no qualms about eating carbs or fat—or too much or too little of this or that. She was just comfortably enjoying her meal. Which was good too because most people would be freaking out over being a real target, as in dead from a hit-and-run at worst or just canned from their job for something they didn't even do at the very least. He admired her for her gumption.

He looked over to see Galen studying them. Johan frowned, and Galen just grinned.

Kai turned and looked around the table at her friends. "Well, obvious undercurrents are going on here," she said. "So, what's going on?"

"He kissed me," Joy snapped. There was silence at the

table.

"Who kissed you?" Kai asked cautiously.

"Johan," Joy said. Then she picked up another bite of her quiche and bit hard. She chewed furiously, her gaze locked on Kai.

Johan's grin was hard to keep back. The other men just looked at him with raised eyebrows. He shrugged and said, "Hey, it seemed like the thing to do at the time."

Maybe that wasn't the right thing to say because immediately Joy turned on him and said, "What?" Her voice was low and ominous.

He gave her a flat stare back, yet his voice faltered at the end. "It seemed like the thing to do at the time?"

She gasped and opened her mouth, just as Kai reached across the table and popped more quiche into it. "We won't fight about it now," she said. "We have to focus on the business at hand."

"You asked," Johan said.

Kai nodded. "I did. I should have known better." She shook her head but turned toward Joy. "All of Levi's men, they're very honorable," she said, "but they are deadly too."

Joy narrowed her gaze, still chewing hard as she glared from Kai to Johan. Finally she seemed to have calmed down enough that she served herself some salad and attacked the green lettuce as if it were an alien enemy.

Johan watched with interest to see her plow through a big serving of greens. Finally he looked at the others and said, "So, what news do you have?"

"It's not even so much news," Tyson said, "but we'll be in town to give you guys a hand. The other job was put on hold. The museum will handle their problem themselves."

At that, Joy stopped chewing, stared at Kai, and said, "I

don't want this to interfere in your life too."

"It's not interfering in my life," Kai said. "We're friends. Remember? I don't want to see you get into trouble."

"I'm already into trouble," she said. "What difference does a little more make?"

"You know what I mean," Kai said. "Let's not be flippant about something like your safety."

Joy seemed to calm down, her shoulders slumping, and she nodded. "There's really nothing to be done though. We're still trying to get to the bottom of it."

"I know," Kai said.

Just then Tyson's phone buzzed. He pulled it out, looked at it, then at Joy. "When did you last have a repairman in your apartment?"

She looked at him in surprise, then frowned and shrugged. "Not sure I've had any. I've hardly lived there long enough."

"Does anybody have a spare key?"

"No," she said. "Well, the guy I sublet it from. But he's overseas. And of course the property manager. Why?"

"Because we sent a team into your apartment and cased it for bugs. They found two."

She stopped and stared at him in shock, slowly lowering her fork. "Bugs, as in listening devices?"

He nodded slowly.

"That's not cool." She gave Galen a blank look. "That makes no sense. Why care about me?"

"Do you leave a spare key anywhere?" Johan asked.

"No," she said. "I just have the one on a key ring I keep in my purse."

"And how often do you leave your office without your purse?" Johan stared at her intently, because, of course, she had come to talk to him several times, and she didn't have her purse with her.

"You're suggesting somebody might have gone into my purse while I was out of the office? So they could do what? So they could take an impression of my key and have another key made?"

"Something like that, yes," he said. "It's possible, isn't it?"

"But that would mean it was either Phyllis or Doris," she said slowly. "I can't see either one of them doing that."

"Johan told us about Phyllis and her interesting history," Kai said.

"Interesting, yes. But surely not something that would necessitate her bugging my apartment," Joy said.

"No, and what I'm trying to ascertain is," she said, "who else would care?"

"Only somebody involved in the theft," Johan said slowly.

Joy looked down at her food. "Suddenly I'm not so hungry. Now I feel quite sick."

Chapter 7

"I DIDN'T MEAN to ruin your dinner," Kai said.

"I'm the one who just got the news," Tyson said apologetically. "I could have waited a little bit."

Joy stared at him in surprise. "Waiting a little bit won't help," she murmured. "This means that strangers were in my apartment, and even now people are trying to hear what I have to say." She looked back at Johan. "Did we say anything when we were in there?"

He shook his head. "No," he said, "deliberately."

She glared at him. "Did you expect there to be bugs?"

"Expect, no," he said. "But I'm the one who requested the sweep."

She stared around at all these people who were making decisions on her behalf without her. Yes, for her benefit, but, at the same time, it felt odd. She didn't even know what to say. She stared off in the distance. "I can't imagine," she reiterated, "why anybody would care."

"And, of course, that's the problem," Kai said. "Like you said, it could only be somebody involved in the theft."

"But that could mean anybody in the whole company," Joy said.

"Or from one of the related companies," Galen added.

"Not to mention some thug hired off the street," Johan said.

"Or maybe the bugs were left behind by the previous tenant," Tyson guessed.

"Except for the opportunity to get a copy of my key." Joy sighed, looking slowly at everyone.

"But you have to take into consideration that any one of us," Galen said, apologetically looking at Joy, "could pick that lock in ten seconds flat."

She wrinkled up her face at him. "Oh, please, not in ten seconds."

"Only ten seconds if we were out of practice," Johan said. "All of us would pride ourselves on doing it in much less time."

She reached up to massage her forehead. "So, can I even go back to my apartment?"

"The team pulled the bugs," Tyson said quietly. "So, for the moment, it's safe in that regard. We could set an alarm so that it triggers a security response at the compound, if somebody opened that door. You may want to find some other place to live in the meantime."

"But then they'll know that I'm on to them," Joy said, "and that can't be very smart either."

"Possibly not," Tyson acknowledged.

"It all sucks," she said.

"It absolutely does."

"So what's the best answer, you guys?" Joy asked. "Is there any way to track those bugs? Find out who placed them in my apartment?"

"No. However, the bugs are on their way to Levi's compound," Tyson said. "We'll do the best we can to see, but they look fairly innocuous, as in anybody could have bought them over the internet."

"And, of course, they don't come with a signature or

anything that says, 'Hey, we did this,' right?"

Johan shook his head and said, "Sorry. You also don't have any video cameras in the apartment building, so there's no way to track if anybody had entered that way."

"I'm on the third floor," she said. "I suppose it wouldn't be all that hard for somebody who's good at this to climb up and get in through the glass doors. But apparently it is pretty easy to get in through the front door, so why bother?"

The men just nodded and continued to eat their dinner.

Making a steeple with her fingers, Joy rested her chin on top of her hands. "It sounds like the best thing would be if I continue to do nothing and let you guys set up whatever it is you're setting up to try to catch the people who did this."

"But we also have to set up something at the company," Tyson said. "This can't be one single prong. Otherwise it won't work."

"We don't even know who at the company is involved," she said. Turning, she looked at Galen and Johan. "Unless you two found something."

Both men shrugged, and Galen said, "Not yet. So far we have those four accounts that have been compromised, and we're still trying to trace the materials sitting in those three locked rooms downstairs in the building—from either end, whether the seller or the buyer."

"And I don't understand that either," she said. "I don't have any record of surplus supplies designated in those three storerooms on Level B3 in my inventory."

"I was checking that just before we left today," Johan said. "None of the numbers that I randomly scanned in match up with any of the inventory online."

"And there are three rooms full?" Kai asked.

"Yes," Johan said. "All different types of materials

though. The last room appears to be medications, like drugs and chemicals."

Kai nodded slowly. "I wonder how old they are, whether they're outdated and stored down there as *out of circulation* or whatever and waiting to be destroyed."

Johan thought about that and shrugged. "That would be good to know. I didn't see anything on the boxes, like labels or expiration dates, but I didn't look that close at all sides of every box."

"We'll probably have to open up some of the cases to see expiration dates on the bottles," Joy said, "because, in reality, that stuff could have been there for a long time."

"As in years or decades?"

"If that part of the building isn't used, it's hard to say," she said. "So who would have access to it is what we need to know."

"I can talk to Edward when we go back tomorrow morning," Johan said. "He came in and reamed us out pretty good because I was talking to the shipping foreman."

"The usual *dig in to cause a stir and shake things up a bit* tactic?" Kai asked with a knowing grin.

Johan gave her a lopsided grin. "Everybody lies when it suits them. Some only reveal the truth when they're shocked."

"So let's really shake them up a bit then," Tyson said. "We might have to get one of our guys assigned to the building too though."

"That would be interesting," Joy said. "I wonder if there's any inspector the new guy could come in as."

"Not likely. Maybe audits though," Johan said. He looked at Kai. "What do you think? Some kind of special investigator?"

She frowned and said, "I don't know one end of a bookkeeping ledger from another," Kai said. "What about health inspectors?"

"There would be no reason for them to be there," Joy said. "No animals are on the premises. But will your fake auditor get access to the secret dark rooms that nobody seems to know anything about?" Joy joked. "Or will the company try to keep any auditor away from everybody and especially Level B3?"

"We'll have to look into that," Tyson said, still texting somebody. "I think we're better to go in as auditors or something that gives us broad access to their computer system. Ice will know what to set our covers up as."

Joy presumed it was his boss, Levi. "So who is paying all your wages?" she asked suddenly. "I don't want you guys getting in trouble for being here."

"We're here with Levi's permission," Kai said.

"So what's in it for him?" she asked.

Kai looked at her, surprised. "That's a very good question. In Levi's case, it's likely for justice. He hates scenarios like this. He has brought up this case with the police to maybe link to Chelsea. So, if it's a murder investigation, it's on everybody's radar."

"But then we'd have the cops in my building," Joy said. "Not health inspectors."

"Well, that's a good point too," Kai said. "Maybe some of Levi's guys could go in as detectives."

"You mean, pretending to be police officers?" Joy said. "That's against the law."

"Not if we have permission from the police," Kai suggested.

"That you won't get," Tyson noted.

"Possibly not."

There was silence as everybody considered what their options were.

"Is there a company above this one?" Kai asked.

"Just the board," Joy said. "This is the umbrella company. I believe a couple companies are under it, one of which used to work at this location as well."

"Used to?"

"Used to," Joy said, "though I'm not exactly sure why I used past tense there. Maybe it is an old defunct company, and maybe the materials in those rooms were leftovers from that business. Although I thought I remembered seeing something about an office supply company, so maybe not in relation to the drugs you found there."

"That would be good to know either way," Kai said, writing down notes. "More conversations for Edward." Kai paused, then asked, "What about the owner-CEO himself?"

"Edward seems to think Barlow's an idiot," Johan said. "I've never met Barlow, but I've seen his board member photo."

"He is not the smartest bulb," Joy said. "I would have said he was slimy but harmless, up until I talked to Phyllis. Now I'm not so sure."

"And how bad does Phyllis feel about all this now?" Kai asked. "Any chance of her being after revenge?"

"It's a long cold day for revenge," Joy said. "But why would she have told me all that history if it was her? That wouldn't have been very astute of her."

"True, but that doesn't mean it's impossible. It's an odd scenario, but we've seen a lot of odd people doing odd things in this world," Johan said.

Joy agreed with that. She sighed. "So, as much as it is

great to see you guys, was this intended as a personal visit or as a business meeting?"

"Both," Kai said, reaching across to grab her friend's fingers and squeeze. "And we wanted to make sure that you were safe."

"Well, I'm safe enough at the moment," she said. "But, if we keep digging through the company, they may start to take steps to protect themselves."

"They're already doing that," Johan said.

"Can you tell that from the accounts?"

"We can tell that from the IT. There's been a lot less activity on the network this past week, now that we're watching, than there was compared to the previous week's IT activity."

"Of course it's expected that some things will stop. People checking in on friends and relatives, going to social media sites that they shouldn't be going to while at work, using other people's accounts, or using other people's log-ins. Things they might do on a regular basis at work become something they don't want to take a chance on now. Not that they have any illegal motivation, just that it's not the best practices and probably against corporate policy, and they don't want to get caught." Joy sighed. "So what do we do from here?" she asked. "It's not just about theft. If you think that Chelsea died because of her job, then this is about murder."

"Yes," Kai said gently. "But how widespread is this? We don't want to cut off one head while the main part of the body is gloating beneath us."

Joy wrinkled up her nose at that thought. "Okay, that sounds pretty ugly. So what do we have to do in order to make sure that we get all of it?"

"It'll take time," Johan said. "It will be a few days before we can get to the bottom of this."

"I hope you're right about that," she said. "I hadn't really planned on quitting my job just now, but obviously I no longer have a choice."

Kai nodded slowly. "And that's one of the reasons why I was hoping maybe we could get you to quit earlier."

"I don't know," she said. "That's a hard thing to do. I don't want to leave it right now. We don't exactly have a reason for it either."

"Maybe not," Kai said, "but making the wrong choice now could have a very bad outcome."

Joy smiled at her friend. "I trust you. I trust all of you. You'll do your best to keep me safe. And, if you guys can't do it, so be it. I sure as hell couldn't do it on my own," she said with a smile.

JOY'S WORDS WERE something that Johan kept close to his heart as he continued his cyberwork Saturday morning from his hotel room. He was frustrated because every time he thought he'd gotten through to another level of the company's intranet system, he kept coming up with more blocks.

He turned to Galen as they worked side by side and asked, "How come we're having so much difficulty getting through everything?"

"I think they're busy putting up firewalls right now," Galen said.

"It's midmorning on a Saturday," Johan said. "That means a ton of people right now are trying to block our ability to get where we want to go."

"And you've got to wonder why."

"Maybe someone on the board of directors could be the hacker and whoever's doing the stealing," Johan said.

"And it could be an otherwise honest loyal employee who disagrees with what Edward and the board have allowed Barlow to do."

"That brings up another point. It could be whoever's against Barlow, Edward, and the company too."

Galen shook his head. "The hackers are not even really trying to hide their tracks, and, if they're asked about it, they'll say that they were asked to boost the security within their company."

"Are you ready for a field trip?" Johan asked, sitting back.

Galen looked at him, smiled, and nodded. "Always. I'm more than done with being on the computer," he said.

Johan stood. "Let's head over and look at the company itself."

"Have we been given permission?" Galen asked.

Grinning, Johan snapped his laptop closed. "Yeah. Edward refused. He's still mad about me talking to the shipping foreman. Finally Barlow caved, once Levi had him on the phone."

"I've just been waiting for you," Galen said, laughing. "Let's go." As he logged off his laptop, Galen then asked, "What about Joy? Will you tell her?"

Johan shrugged. "She'll just want to come along."

"True enough. I'd suggest you send her a text to make sure she's doing okay though."

"Kai stayed overnight," he said, "and Tyson. I'm sure Joy's fine." Nevertheless he grabbed his phone and quickly sent her a text. **Heading out to do more intel work. Just wanted to make sure you're okay.**

I'm fine. We're about to sit down to brunch.

Good enough. I'll contact you later.

He pocketed his phone, nodded at Galen, and they walked out of their hotel room. They were just ten minutes away from the company.

As they walked in, using their passes on the side door, he noted that the place sounded like a morgue. "Weird how office buildings are so empty on weekends," he said.

"And yet I wonder how empty this one is."

They headed to their workspace, hooked up their laptops, and started searching online to see if anybody was around.

"I'm into the security system," Johan said. "Two cards were accessed at noon, which were ours, and two were accessed this morning."

"Where are they now?"

"One is Barlow. He's up in his office. He's supposedly still there, but I don't know that for certain. I don't have an ID on the other one. It just says, *visitor pass.*"

"Did he come in with Barlow?"

"Within a few minutes."

"So that person could be with him, or it could be someone who followed behind him."

"I know," he said. "First things first, let's go find Barlow and see if he's even here."

"And the reason?" Galen asked. They took their laptops with them and headed toward the elevator.

"We're here to investigate crimes," he said. "Do we need another excuse?"

Galen shrugged. "Not really," he said, "but it would be nice if we had something that we could pinpoint. Pretty quickly they will all look at us as wasting everybody's time."

"I know," he said. "We could say the same thing about them too."

They rode up the elevator and finally stopped on the top floor. When they stepped out, once again that empty hollow sound permeated the area. They walked down to Barlow's office and rapped on the door. When there was no answer, Johan turned the handle, but it was locked. Johan frowned, asking Galen, "Did he come out of his office?"

"No," Galen said, frowning as he checked. "It says he's still in here."

Johan pulled out his card and used it to unlock the door, only it wouldn't unlock. "Once again we don't have security override to enter everywhere," he said. Pulling out his lockpick set, he had the door opened in a few seconds.

"Now that set off an alarm," Galen said. He worked on his laptop, holding it with one hand, shutting down the alarm with the other.

"Good enough." Johan pushed open the door and called out, "Barlow, are you here?"

There was no answer.

They were in what appeared to be a large reception area with a couple private offices farther inside. "So this is like a private suite," Johan muttered.

Galen sat in the front room, still working on his laptop.

Johan walked through the reception area, headed toward what was the biggest office in the corner. He didn't need to look far because Barlow was right here on the floor. "Damn." Barlow stared at Johan, but no life was left in his eyes. A bullet hole decorated his forehead. *Looks like a .22 made entry. A woman's gun usually*, Johan thought. *But don't get trapped into that thinking.*

"Damn," Johan whispered. "This case just got much uglier."

Chapter 8

W HEN THE PHONE call came to her cell an hour later, the two other phones in her apartment went off as well. Joy looked at Kai and Tyson as they all reached for their phones.

"Johan, what's up?" Joy asked.

"The CEO of the company—Barlow—he's dead," he said. "Two security cards accessed the building this morning. His was one of them."

"What?" she cried out. "That's terrible. How did you find him?" she asked, her hand over her chest as she thought about the ramifications. "Was it a heart attack?"

"Possibly, but it went hand in hand with a bullet then too," he snapped.

"He was murdered?" She bounced up to her feet.

She and Kai had been sitting here, nursing the second pot of coffee, talking about everything—from Kai's relationship with Tyson, Joy's relationship with Johan, which she'd called a *nonrelationship*—all as Tyson worked in the living room. They'd shared a wonderful brunch of pancakes, and, when that was over, things had fallen to the side of girl talk. But now all three of them were on their phones.

"This is just too unbelievable," Joy said. "I wonder why?"

"We did a quick search of his office," Johan said, "but

we didn't find anything else."

"Who was the other security card?" she asked.

"It was a visitor's pass," Johan replied.

"You should be able to check the log to see who it was signed out to."

"Okay, hold on a sec." When he came back on the line, he said, "Galen's checking."

After a few seconds, she heard Galen say something in the background to Johan.

"Jesus," said Johan. "It literally says Donald Duck."

She stopped pacing and froze. "Are you serious?"

"Yeah. Quack-quack," he said in disgust.

"So Barlow likely came in with his killer."

"That would make sense, yes," he said. "We're thinking that, chances are, he was followed to work, and this person came in right behind him."

"That makes sense," she said, "unless it was somebody he knew."

"We're also looking at the security cameras, but guess what?"

"What?" she asked, her heart sinking.

"All the cameras were offline this morning."

"Oh, good Lord," she said. "So, it was a setup, and he was definitely targeted."

"Which means everybody in the company is now in danger—as well as a potential suspect."

"And yet," she said, "it still doesn't make any sense."

"It will," he said, his voice grim. "We just don't know all the details yet."

"So, what do you want me to do?"

"Stay safe. Stay there with Kai and Tyson."

Joy took a deep breath. "Fine, I'll be careful," she said. "I feel safe here."

"How can you feel safe," he said, "when you know that your place was bugged?"

"But that's past tense," she said, "it isn't now. Besides, Kai and Tyson are here. *Past* meaning that I don't want to think about it."

"Not wanting to think about it doesn't change anything," he snapped.

"Makes no sense right now." She took several slow deep breaths, the tension in his voice catching her attention. "What do you want me to do?" she asked.

"I want you to stay alive. That's what I want you to do."

"And you? You could have a murderer in that building right now."

"We're counting on it," he snapped, and he hung up. She slowly put down her phone to see the other two staring at her. "I presume you heard the news?"

They both nodded. "Yes," Kai said. "The cops will be there any second, if they're not already. Johan and Galen are searching the building, and the members of the board of directors are being contacted."

"Right. A whole investigation kicks into gear now, I suppose."

Kai paced around the room. "The real question is, who would want him dead?"

"Well, if he's the slimy asshole I believe him to be," Joy said, "the real question is, who *wouldn't* want him dead?"

"A huge suspect pool, great. That won't help," Tyson said.

"I believe over 240 people work for the umbrella company, so that's not an enormous pool but big enough." She stopped, stared, her mind obviously working overtime.

"Honestly, even though I kinda like the woman for her tenacity, I'd have to put Phyllis at the top of the list."

"You don't believe her when she says she doesn't care anymore?"

"I don't know," Joy said. "It would be hard for me to continue working there."

"Got it," Tyson said, "but you're different from everybody else, and people have all kinds of reasons for doing what they do."

"I get that," she said, "but still, I'd be checking into her whereabouts."

"That's for the police to do," he said. "Again we were officially kicked out of that investigation as well. So we'll do an unofficial investigation. I'm waiting for Johan and Galen to complete a full search on the building."

"Will that do any good?"

"Yes," he said. "It will."

She shook her head. "But why? The cops are there now. They'll take over, and this person can either hide or disappear in the chaos."

"Which is exactly what the murderer would do, but the guys have got the security cameras back up."

She stopped staring, and a slow smile filled her face. "Well now, that makes sense," she said. "What they need to do is find a central location and stand in place, until they see who is moving through the building."

"They're already on it."

She nodded. "Of course Johan didn't tell me any of that."

"Of course not," Kai said. "But then you two seemed to be at odds."

"I don't know what we're at," she said, frowning, because she wished she was at the building with him. There was just something very comforting and solid about him. It's not like any of this chaos in her life would happen if he was here full-time. And yet she had no way to know if that were even true and less reason to believe it. It was foolish to even think such a thing, but that was how she felt. It had likely come from that quiet sense of power he exuded. That competency and that sense of having everything under control. It felt like nothing in her life had been under control since she had moved here. She'd been totally okay for the adventure of planning to relocate, expecting everything to go her way, but, when she'd had such trouble finding a decent job, panic had set in, and she had ended up at Westgroup. It wasn't what she wanted to do; it wasn't what she expected, and, now that she was here, it seemed like it would be even harder to find another position. She sagged into place.

Kai walked over, gave her a quick hug, and said, "They'll be okay, you know?"

"There's a killer in the building," Joy said. "I don't know that anybody's safe."

"Well, he won't stick around," Tyson said. "That you can count on."

"I hear you," she said. "It just feels like everything took a giant leap backward. This isn't what I wanted when I signed up for this job. And, when I contacted you, all I was concerned about was the fact that drugs could be on the street that could be dangerous."

"There *are* drugs on the street that are dangerous," Kai said quietly. "Even more now. But I suspect what we have here is a very sophisticated system of moving drugs through the company in a way that nobody knows about, except for a few select people."

"And you think Barlow could have been one of them?"

"As the founder, he certainly could have been the one to set it up," Tyson said, "but we don't know that for sure."

"Right," she said. "Well, he's dead now, so there'll be a lot of changes at the company."

"And again you have to consider the fact that you may not necessarily have a job."

"Right. Although what does any of that have to do with me?"

"You're the low man on the totem pole," Tyson said. "If the board cuts the budget, that'll be the first place where they'll start—with the new hires—leaving the old-timers with seniority in place."

"Great," she said. "That doesn't seem fair." She stared grimly out the window. "I should be okay for a few months," she said, "but I'll have to get another job right away."

"THERE," GALEN SAID. "Looks like somebody just went through one of the doors to the shipping yards."

Johan walked to the laptop and took a closer look. "I'll go down there," he said. "Stay connected to my cell phone. You keep tracking our suspect and let me know when I'm getting close."

"Will do," Galen said. "We'll have to tell the cops too."

"We'll tell the cops if and when we find something," he said.

He stepped out of their small dingy office and headed in the direction of the door that had just opened and closed. It meant somebody was here, was still inside the building, and Johan wanted to know who it was and why they were here. If it was one of the cops, then the cops would have said something. Most likely anyway. But then again, it shouldn't have been just one cop, and Galen or Johan should have seen somebody in uniform on the security feed. Instead, it was just a momentary blip on their security screen, noting the door had opened, and that was it. No chance to catch sight of anybody in the area. But then, as he remembered, not many cameras were down there.

He raced down the stairway and down to the hallway, going the long way around past the three locked doors and out to the small extra stairway that led up to the shipping dock. As he stopped there, he quickly texted Galen. **I'm outside the shipping bays, coming from the B3 stairwell up to B2. Any sign?**

No. But check out the east side of the building. Seems to be one of the side doors into the shipping bay. Yet looks like maybe it leads to an office.

I'll check.

He pulled open the door and stepped inside. The shipping bay was in darkness, and it took a moment for his eyes to adjust. He studied the layout, still seeing all the heavy equipment. The big bay doors were closed and locked, so the main part of the floor was empty, except for a tiny sliver of light on the far side.

He raced across and headed toward the office. He could see the light coming from the inside, and, with an ear against the door, he could hear a voice. But only one, so it was likely he was talking on the phone. He quickly sent a text message to Galen about it and got a quick reply.

You going in?

I am.

He turned the doorknob and stepped inside.

The shipping foreman looked up at him in shock and then anger. "What are you doing here again?" he snapped.

"I told you that we would be here this weekend," he said mildly.

The foreman stood, his hands on his hips. "Everything's fucking changed now," he said.

"Why is that?"

"I'm sure you know about the dead guy here."

"You mean the owner of the company? And how did you know about him so soon?"

"The police scanned my truck's license plates, sitting out on the lot here. The cop called me, demanding to know what I'm doing here. Telling me to sit tight and how a uniform will be down to interrogate me."

"So who do you think did this? Someone who wanted the penthouse suite?"

"Hell no. Barlow's only a figurehead," he snapped. "He hasn't had enough shares to make a vote go his way in a very long time."

"Not a lot of people liked him apparently."

"What's to like? He was scum."

"You feel pretty strongly about it."

The foreman shrugged and stared at the door behind him. "How many other people are here?"

"The place is teeming with cops," Johan said. "To be expected when a murderer is still on the premises."

The foreman sat down with a heavy *thud*. "Of all the damn days to come in to get caught up on the paperwork."

"Yeah, it would be much better if you were at home with an alibi," Johan said.

"What about you?" he asked. "How come you're not at home with an alibi?"

"Me and my partner found the body," Johan said. "That changes things for us too."

The foreman snorted. "Of course," he said. "It doesn't mean you're not guilty. Maybe you two killed him and then called the cops?"

"Maybe," Johan said, "but nope."

"Chances are none of us will have a job now," the foreman said.

"Why is that?"

"Because the board wants to sell the company. They've had a couple offers over the past few years, and Barlow was always against it."

"But he didn't have enough votes to stop it, you said."

"No, but he had some friends on the board. Still doesn't mean with him gone that anybody'll give a shit."

"And does selling the company really make a difference?" Johan asked. "When you think about it, often sales or takeovers are good for a company."

"Sure, but it also means shuffling a lot of the staff around, so chances are I won't have a job."

"That's pretty defeatist thinking," Johan said quietly, as he looked around. "Do you know of anything criminal going on here?"

"No," he said. "Why would I?"

"I don't know that you would," he said. "I'm just wondering. Something crazy had to be going on because, for that murder to have happened, there's got to be a motive. If something was going on, it's possible that Barlow found out and approached the person."

"Barlow didn't approach anybody," he said. "He didn't give a shit. And, if you paid him in scotch, he'd turned a blind eye. You could have stolen this place blind, and he wouldn't have cared."

At that, Johan pulled a seat up and said, "Tell me more."

The foreman glared at him. "Why should I?"

"To save your job," he said.

"And maybe it's time to leave." His shoulders sagged. "My wife's been on me to retire anyway."

"Do you like working here that much?"

"No," he said, "but I'm bored stiff at home, so having a job of some kind makes me feel like I'm not quite so old."

Johan had heard that before from other men. "Got it," he said. "But, in situations like this one, it can get ugly."

"It can, indeed," he said frowning. "Look. I've known Barlow for over twenty years. The guy's an asshole, free and clear. When the board of directors took over, they pretty well left him as a figurehead because he started the company, and it's his face everywhere. But he never did. At least not since he became successful."

"What does he do with his days then?"

"I think he played video games and went golfing, for all I know. I don't care," he said. "The company operated just fine without him, and, with any luck, it will now too."

"You just said everything would change."

"And I'm hoping maybe I'll be wrong," he said.

"Anything else you can tell me?"

The foreman sat back and crossed his arms over his chest. "It doesn't matter what I say. Anything I say will sound like it's just sour grapes at this point."

"Unless you know about the theft that's been going on here."

"Is there any going on?"

"Not only is there but it's also coming through your area here. So either you're heavily involved or somebody's using you as a patsy."

The foreman's eyebrows shot up. "Hell no," he said.

"I've worked for the company since forever. There hasn't been any theft that I know of in all that time."

"So either you're being duped, or you're really foolish and don't want to see what's right before your eyes."

"I don't like what you're implying," the foreman said, standing now. "I don't have anything to do with any theft here, and neither do any of my guys."

"What's with the three rooms full of stored goods just around the corner?" Johan pointed the direction of the rooms to him.

The foreman looked in that direction and frowned. "That shit's been there since forever," he said. "It was part of the other company."

"What other company?"

"That was Barlow's deal too. He was struggling to get some of the stock he needed, so he bought a company that would allow him to import larger amounts of it at one time. But he couldn't get credit, overextended himself, and ended up going broke. And most of the stock that he had here, for whatever bloody reason, he didn't even ship out."

"So it's all just wasted old merchandise?"

"And that happens more than you think," he said. "I got a buddy who did something similar. He started a business and had a ton of stock stored. He didn't have room, so he moved the stuff off the premises, couldn't pay his bills, and ended up losing everything. The lenders came in, taking what they could, selling it for pennies on the dollar. When he turned around a few years later, he remembered he'd put a truckload of stuff in a couple storage lockers that he'd paid for with cash because he needed another place back then. Yet now it had all gone past its expiration dates."

"And why did he do that?"

"Because he got in over his head and didn't think about it. He was just looking for short-term answers. It went to pot, and he figured that for sure the contents of the storage lockers would be taken too. He was just so angry, he let the creditors do whatever they would do and signed the papers to be done with it. He got the bills later for the two storage lockers, that he'd paid upfront for three years, cash money, and it had come due again. He went over there, took one look, and found all that shit was still there."

"Damn. Did he sell it?"

"He did, and then he got in trouble because, according to the paperwork he'd signed, he hadn't declared the contents of those storage lockers."

"So it's possible that the stuff is sitting here because nobody knows what to do with it?"

"Makes sense to me," he said. "And, depending on how much theft you're talking about, it'd be pretty easy to move a bunch of boxes in and out of those rooms, and nobody would know because really nobody has any idea what's in there to begin with."

"So somebody could have completely switched out those boxes, and nobody would have known?"

He shrugged. "Yep. But it's got nothing to do with me."

"Unless the boxes come in here through you."

He frowned at that. "If they come in through here, then it's just straight inventory that's either coming here for additional storage—because we have a warehouse already for the research center—and then they're being shipped back out again."

"Ah, so you do ship to the research center?"

"Yes," he said. "We have most of our product come here because we don't have enough space at the other place to hold everything."

"That makes sense. But didn't you tell me earlier, if it comes in on a truck, it might as well go to the intended destination?"

"Sure, for this company, in this building, but the research center is under a different company name. It's typical. They have an umbrella company, and they have companies under it," he said. "I just get the orders in and put the shit where it belongs per the address on the shipping label."

"Does this building have different sections by company?"

"For bookkeeping purposes and deducting the utilities, yes," he said. "But, as far as we're concerned, it's not a big issue. I keep everything over here for the research center." He pointed behind him. "Off to the side is stuff for this company."

"How many other companies are there?"

"Two more, but one is a property management company, and I don't get stuff for them delivered here," he said. "I don't even know what the other company does. Again I don't deal with that."

"So you have rooms and rooms of stuff for the research center?"

"Sure. Come on. I'll show you." He got up and headed to the office door.

Chapter 9

J OY LOOKED OVER at Kai. "Is there anything constructive we can do while Johan and Galen are at the office?"

"Like what?" Kai asked curiously.

Joy bounced to her feet and paced back and forth in her small living room. "I don't know," she said, "but it feels wrong to have started the whole ball rolling and now be completely cut out and not effective at doing anything."

"Well, the guys are doing something," she said, "and that's what happens. You initiate something like this, and people who are pros step in and take over."

Kai's voice was calm and practiced, as if she'd spoken to many an irate woman before. Joy looked at her with a lopsided grin. "You're very good at what you do."

"What is it that I do anyway?" Kai asked, concern in her voice. "It seems like I'm split between my own company— inventing and designing military-grade training equipment—and Levi's outfit."

"I guess because you're with Tyson that it's hard to not go on some missions, or at least want to go on some, yet still be pulled in the other direction."

"Exactly," she said. "Some of the stuff the guys are coming up with depends on us, and we're really excited about developing it. And, while I'm sitting here, I'm looking at designs, and a couple more of them have been emailed to me that I hadn't had a chance to even go over yet." She looked at Tyson, his face buried in the laptop. "He, on the other hand, is probably digging up dirt on everybody who works at your company."

Tyson didn't respond, but the corners of his mouth kicked up.

Joy took that as a yes. "I need more coffee," she said.

"You need less caffeine," Kai said in a dry tone.

She looked at her friend and asked, "You want to go for a walk then? I'm bouncing around this small space, and I can't do anything."

"Absolutely," she said. "How about we do a loop around the park? Do you have any shopping you need to do?"

She shrugged, looked around, and said, "We don't have anything for dinner."

"We can go out," Tyson said. "Or order in."

"Or we could buy groceries," Joy said. "I don't mind cooking."

"It might give you something else to think about," Kai said. "Come on. Let's go." The women quickly had shoes and sweaters on. Kai turned to look at Tyson, who stared at them steadily. She shrugged and said, "We'll just go together, if you're okay with that."

He gave a slow nod. "Stay in touch."

Kai walked over, bent down, and kissed him thoroughly.

Joy watched with envy because, not only did Kai have that well-loved look on her face all the time but, by the time she stepped back, Tyson did too. Kai sighed happily as they stepped out.

"It's really good to see you two guys so happy like that."

"Sure, but it took time," she said. "Remember? It was a pretty rocky road at the beginning."

"Has he gotten over the death of his wife and daughter?"

"Does anybody ever get over that?" Kai countered. "It has to be dealt with, as much as he can, of course. Is he happier and much more content to move on? Yes. Does he love me now? Yes."

"I guess that's what I was asking, clumsily though," Joy said with a laugh. "I don't want him to be pining for a woman who can't come back, then cheating you out of a relationship."

"No," she said. "I can grieve with him because she was my first best friend. There was just nothing anybody could do."

They looped arms as they headed out toward the park about a block away. "Outside of the mess at work," Kai said, "how are you settling into Houston?"

"It's okay," she said. "It's definitely warmer than where I was, and I'm happy with that, but I really liked the work I used to do. This is just a stop-gap job. It's just a paycheck," she said with a shrug.

"And a lot of people only ever get that paycheck job," Kai said. "They're happy to have it. But you want something more."

"I do, yes," she said. "I want to have something like what I had—or another purpose. It's okay to go to work and help somebody else's company run smoothly, but it would be better, in my case, if I had something that I was achieving. I didn't realize how success-oriented I was, and being here has shown me that I don't really want to let go of something once I dig it up. Whether it was an issue in processes or details of a case or a possible crime, part of me just wants to get in as deep as I can and figure it out."

"That's the puzzle solver in you," Kai said, laughing. "It

would have been nice if you'd found something like a really crappy process you could fix instead of a theft. Particularly a theft of drugs."

"It has always bothered me that *theft* was considered almost on a gradient scale. Like, maybe a stolen pen was nothing. If you stole a pad of paper from the office, it was nothing. If you stole a partial pack of printer paper, it was nothing because the pack was opened anyway. You know? Things like that? But it amazes me, as I've gone through a few companies now, just how much all that adds up to. Although the company itself doesn't like it, the employees often don't even worry about it and take it almost as if it's their due. I've seen people steal coffee filters, tea bags, saying, 'The corporation can afford it. I can't.' Everything from office supplies to toilet paper," she said with a bewildered look. "And you know the office toilet tissue is never very nice and soft."

"I can't imagine, as an employee, doing that to the person who signs my paycheck," Kai said. "And from the employer side, I have my own company, plus I see Levi's company. I can't imagine employee theft at either place. Not with the people we hire. They are all a cut above the rest."

"And yet it probably happens."

Kai shook her head. "At Levi's place it doesn't happen, because their mind-set is, if you need it, take it," she said. "And I've tried to emulate that level of trust in my own company."

"Is that working out?"

"It is. Granted, we hire the best. They work odd hours at odd locations. So taking a pad and a pen to the local park to sketch out the cityscape to invent ways for our military to get inside buildings and to stop others from gaining entry is all part of their job. If it's office supplies, I consider it already used. So, if they take a pad home, I don't care. I don't expect them to be doodling on napkins from restaurants or their paper towels at home," she said. "To me, it all comes out in the wash. Granted, I bet we have such a low percentage of such internal 'thefts,' that it would hardly be measurable. Still, I know a lot of companies don't look at employee theft that way. Probably because they're not hiring the right people, who are then stealing from them. So sad."

"And it's never a good thing when it comes to drugs."

"No. That is not allowed anywhere. Especially something like ketamine," she said thoughtfully. "I mean, they use that stuff to knock out a horse. So vets would have it. Any medical supply house would have it. Pharmaceutical companies and pharmacies would have it. It's also a common drug used by serial killers and rapists," she said, "because it pretty well knocks out the victim."

"But it's different from roofies though, right?"

"Yes, much stronger," Kai said. "Though, once it's on the street, there is no way anyone can really know what they've got."

They wandered around the small pond, stopping to admire the ducks, the sunshine, and the bright flowers. "It's a nice area," Kai said.

"It is, but it's still busy out here," she said. "I should have moved to the outskirts area, so it would be more country instead of this suburbia feel."

"The thing about suburbia is that everybody gets to live there but must work somewhere else," she said. "At least you're working and living close to the same area, so you don't have so far to commute."

"I could technically walk to work if I wanted to," Joy

said. "And, maybe come bad weather, I would, if the driving was treacherous."

"Well, it would save you on car costs."

"And I did consider that," she said. "But there are just enough mornings that I'm late, making me think I'd end up running half the way there."

Kai chuckled. "And here I've been looking at increasing my morning runs," she said.

"But you were always into fitness and weapons and self-defense and martial arts," Joy said. "How come we're friends, since we're complete opposites?"

"Maybe that's why? Opposites attract and all that. I think you are the prettier version of me," Kai said.

"I think you're damn beautiful," Joy said quietly.

"Yeah, see? And you're blind too." The two women laughed and hugged each other.

They had been friends for a long time, having come together at an odd moment in a hotel at a conference that Kai was attending. Joy was attending a conference as well but different events within the same venue. Yet they had clicked immediately and had stuck ever since.

"Any thoughts about you and Tyson having a family?"

"We've talked about it," Kai admitted. "I'm not sure he's ready, and I'm not sure I'm ready."

"No need to rush it anyway," Joy said. "At least you're on that pathway, and, when you're ready, that time will come."

"What about you?" Kai said. "Any boyfriend on the horizon?"

"Nope. Nobody here yet. I thought maybe there would be someone at the company, though I don't really like office romances, and, so far, I haven't seen anybody interesting anyway. Of course I'm stuck in my dungeon," she said in a joking manner.

"I did hear about the lovely working conditions."

"And it's relatively new apparently," she said, "if what Phyllis said is true."

"Meaning that Chelsea was there before you but not anybody else?"

"Yes. Whoever was at the company before Chelsea worked upstairs."

"I wonder if she started something."

"If she did, somebody finished it for her," Joy said starkly. "For no other reason, I'd like to get her some justice, at least."

"And yet it may not be related."

"It may not be," Joy said, "but it would be a hell of a coincidence." And the two exchanged glances because that topic had been a point of conversation time and time again. Neither of them believed in coincidences.

OUT IN THE hallway the foreman turned and looked around. He frowned. "Did you turn on those lights?" He motioned at the back corner.

"No," Johan said, pointing to the stairway door he'd come in through. "I came from over there."

The foreman looked in that direction, shook his head, and said, "That door should be locked. Nobody comes up there."

"Well, three rooms are full of stock in there."

"That's the old stuff, I told you. They are all labeled for the old companies. Hell, I don't even know how many of those companies are even still solvent. For all I know, they shut them all down. Nobody tells me nothing."

It was all Johan could do to hold his smile at that phrase because he'd heard it time and time again from more than a few disgruntled employees. He followed the older man down to the back corner where the light was on. He studied the area. "What about security? Do you have cards that let you know what room everybody's gone into?"

"Nah. It would be a waste of time down here," he said. "We're constantly all over the place."

"It might be a good idea though," he suggested.

"Company's got no money for security down here. Stuff comes in, gets moved around, and stuff goes out. We don't know what's in anything, and we don't care. And, by that token, as long as the stuff comes in, and they have access to it all, the company doesn't care either."

Johan kept his thoughts to himself. It was also pretty obvious that it was a weak system and offered more than a few areas for people to take advantage of, but it wasn't his company, so whatever. He kept his thoughts to himself as he followed the man through the darkened warehouse. Enough daylight and other lighting filtered through that he could see everything that needed to be seen, but it wasn't under a bright light.

He checked the lights up above and noted open rafters with walkways were above them. "Do you ever need the catwalks up there?"

The foreman looked up and shuddered. "I hate heights," he said. "You wouldn't catch me on any catwalk."

Johan nodded but studied the catwalks. "How do you even get up there?"

The foreman pointed to a ladder against the firewall.

"Why were they put up?"

"Something to do with whatever was going on in this building before this company moved in."

"This company didn't build the building?"

"Nah, they took it over. Some big warehouse was in here. I don't remember what."

"I can't imagine why they'd want a catwalk," Johan said.

"Only if they've got a hoist or something up there and may need to do maintenance on it."

"That makes sense," Johan replied, and he could see the relics of something up there. If he checked it out himself later, he wanted Galen around to watch his back when he did. There was definitely a sense of something wrong in this building. Particularly on the weekend.

As they walked up to where the light was on, the foreman snorted and flipped the switch. "This place has ghosties."

"Maybe. But maybe it's just got *people*," he muttered. The foreman shot him a hard look. Johan shrugged. "Most of the time lights are turned on by people."

"Most of the time doesn't mean all the time." And, with that, he led the way down the hallway to another section of the building that Johan had yet to be in.

When he opened the first door, he said, "This is where we used to store a bunch of stuff for the one company. But it's all empty, as you can see."

Johan stepped inside, took a look, and, indeed, the room was empty.

They went down that side for another couple of doorways. All empty. Johan wondered why the foreman was showing him where everything was empty, instead of where the stuff was stashed. But that changed soon.

But then they entered another section, and he said, "In

this huge room here, that wall opens up and joins to the warehouse, so it's easy to access when we have to move stuff in and out of here." And, indeed, there were a lot of boxes and crates.

"What is all this stuff?"

"None of my business," the foreman snapped. He spat onto the floor. "And, if you're smart, you'll remember that. Because it's none of your business either."

Chapter 10

B Y THE TIME the two women stepped out of the nearby grocery store, they were carrying bags of groceries, laughing, and enjoying themselves. Joy couldn't recall having so much fun in quite a long while.

"If you moved to the outskirts of town," Kai said impulsively, "you could be even closer to us."

"Possibly," she said. "I don't have anything in Houston to keep me here in this apartment, but the thought of another move—ugh."

"We could help though."

Joy looked at her friend and smiled. "Are you volunteering Tyson without even asking him?"

"Absolutely," she said with a big grin. "Anything that makes me happy, he's all up for. And to have you closer would definitely make me happy."

Joy was touched. "It is nice to see you," she said. "I hadn't realized how lonely I was starting to feel."

"And that's just as much about your work situation as anything," Kai said. "There's nothing like finding out something nasty is brewing under your nose and how you're caught in the middle of it, all making you feel isolated. Hopefully now that we're here and involved, you don't feel quite the same."

"No," she said, "I definitely don't. And to have Johan

and Galen in the office all the time, well, that's a help too."

"Have you made any friends at work?"

She shook her head. "Not really. The two women I work with in the same room are both odd ducks, and nothing really connects us. Nothing even connects those two, and they've both worked there longer than I have. But, for sure, there's no click between me and either of them, not even a natural friendship. We're coworkers, and that's it."

Kai nodded. "Sometimes it's better that way, but, if you could meet other people in other departments, it would not impact your day-to-day life so much."

"I thought about working at it a little harder," she said, "but first I was focused on making a success of the job so I could pay the rent. And since this all started, I've been so worried about what I'd stepped into. Now, just so much is going on that I'm not sure I want to know anybody else. Apparently I'm in danger, and that could mean anybody around me is in danger too," she said, looking pointedly at Kai.

"Well, it's not like Tyson and I would step out of the way of danger," Kai said comfortably. "This is who we are."

"But it's him who does this kind of work."

"Yes," Kai said, "but I've helped train these men too. Some of the new equipment that we have created is now out with Levi's group, who puts it to the heavy test, and then we make modifications before it goes commercial."

"And does that work out for you?"

"It works out really well. Nothing like having twenty tough men and women to try out and to break in your prototypes so you can improve them. If they can survive Levi's group, I suspect they'll survive World War III."

"Something I hope we never have to go through," Joy

whispered. Back at her apartment, as they walked up the stairs, she said, "You don't realize how much the groceries weigh until you make it home."

"We bought a little more than we expected, I think," Kai said. "And we meant it about going out for dinner or even ordering in."

"Doesn't matter if you did or not," Joy said. "We bought steaks for dinner, so we might as well stay and have them."

"Or you'd have plenty of meals for yourself," Kai argued.

Joy shot her friend a look. "Am I that bad of a cook?"

Just as they walked in, Kai started to laugh and laugh. "Even if you were a magnificent chef, I doubt the guys would let you touch the steaks. And, if you don't have a barbecue grill, I'm not sure they'll be too happy about steaks cooked any other way."

"Steaks need to be barbecued," Tyson said immediately, as he stood up, gathering the bags from their arms and placing them on the counter.

"Well, I don't have a grill," she said.

"Interesting," he said. "Why did you get steaks then?" He gave her a pointed look, as if to say it was completely useless to buy steaks and not have a barbecue grill.

She sighed. "Fine. So maybe we are going out then."

"We could try it in a skillet," he said, "but, depending on the size of the steaks, it'll take a lot of fry pans."

"We could broil them," she said hopefully.

An ominous silence took over her kitchen before Kai chuckled. "Maybe you should look at going out and getting a charcoal barbecue set for Joy," she said to Tyson.

"Or a real one," he said.

"I can't afford anything," Joy said. "I still need all my

paychecks just for survival at the moment, particularly if another move and/or lack of a job is about to rear its head again."

"Right," he said. "We can ask the guys too."

"Ask the guys what?" Kai questioned.

"Have you heard from them?" Joy asked, as she pulled out the groceries. "I didn't even think of them," she said, grimacing. "I've only got four steaks here, no wait, three," she said, frowning.

"Which is what I mean. Put them away, and you'll have three meals for yourself," Kai said gently. "We can hardly not feed Johan and Galen."

"And I guess half a steak won't do much for them, will it?" she asked, staring down at the steaks doubtfully.

"Nope, not likely," Tyson said. "Honestly, with steaks this size, they'd need two apiece anyway."

She looked at him in shock. "Seriously?"

Kai laughed. "Yeah, absolutely."

"Why didn't you say anything?"

"Because this was already costing you a bunch, and you wouldn't let me pay," she said. "So I figured this would be meals for you over the next week or so. After that, you may not even have a job, and you'll be happy to have something on hand."

Frowning, Joy pulled out stuff for sandwiches. "How about a sandwich while we wait for the guys to show up?"

"I could eat," Tyson said immediately.

Kai sighed. "You ate enough brunch for two people," she muttered.

"Your point?"

Kai shook her head and told Joy, "If you haven't been feeding men lately, honest to God, it's brutal."

"Sounds like it," Joy said, "but I can handle sandwiches."

"Good enough," she said.

"And, yes, the guys will be here in another hour or so," Tyson said.

She looked at him. "Did they find anything?"

He shrugged. "Nothing more than they expected."

"That's too bad," she said. "I know it's been a pretty rough day for them already, but you would hope that there would be answers at the end of it."

"There will be," Kai said solemnly. "The thing is, you're just not at that day yet."

JOHAN MET UP with Galen and said, "So I didn't see anything. You didn't either, did you?"

"Nope, outside of that foreman, you didn't meet anyone else down there."

"No, I didn't, and it's possible it was him, but he was in the office, so justifiably in his own space."

"Any reason as to why he was there?"

"Came in to get caught up on paperwork," he said. "My guess is he doesn't much like being home alone with the wife. She nags at him to retire, and he's terrified that's his future."

"Well, he might not get a choice after this scenario," Galen said. "It should be interesting to see the fallout from the murder."

"And no security cameras to say who came in at any time, right?"

"No identity to the one man who came in behind him, if that's what you're asking. Visitor pass to one Donald Duck, as we learned earlier, but no sign of his face appearing on any of the cameras because they were down."

"So were the camera systems down when he got here?"

Galen shook his head. "Not sure. Looks to me like maybe he took them down remotely at some point. Either that or he's sophisticated enough to edit out his entry and stitch clear time back in without it being detected. Or he knew where the cameras were," he said, "and mapped out his pathway with minimal exposure, until he could get in here and take down the cameras."

"Are you ready to go?"

"Nothing more we can do here," he said. "I've downloaded some files that I didn't understand at first glance, and I don't have time to look at them here," Galen said. "So we'll go through them when we get back to the hotel."

"We're going to Joy's place," Johan said. "Kai and Tyson are there. Remember?"

"Right," he said, "we can do it there too then." He stood, and they quickly locked up everything as it should be and walked out.

"I wish we could figure out if anybody is coming in and accessing this room we're using as our temporary office here," Johan said.

"Well, we can certainly set it to see if anybody comes in after us, but you know the police should be doing a full search."

"Yeah, but I highly doubt they will," he said. "Not to this extent. It's a huge building. They'll do a full sweep and won't find anybody. At any locked doors, they'll kick them in, and that'll be the end of it."

"Probably," he said. "There are still a lot of places besides that."

"You're not kidding. I didn't realize they had a catwalk in the shipping dock area."

"I wonder what that's for," Galen said.

"Apparently it's been there since before that foreman's been here. And it does look like some hoses are up on the top."

"So then it would be a catwalk for access?"

"Exactly."

The two men walked out of the building, where a police officer walked over to greet them. As soon as they explained who they were, they were cleared to leave.

He stopped a few feet away from the officer, turned back, and said, "Has anybody else come out?"

The officer shook his head. "No, nobody came by since I've been stationed here."

"Okay," he said and gave Galen a sharp look as they headed to their vehicle. "So does that mean the guy who came in with Barlow left before us or is he still in the building?"

"Could be either," he said. "But without bringing in heat-seeking equipment, which they can hardly justify in a situation like this, we won't know."

"Well, let's take a drive around the parking lot to see who and what's around here, if anything," Johan said. "You realize it also means the foreman's still here."

Frowning, Galen thought about it as he drove and pulled up beside the officer and said, "You know the foreman is still in the shipping area, right?"

The officer frowned, made a note of it, and thanked him.

They pulled around and checked out the other parking lots and found an older midsize truck parked not far from the shipping docks. Johan wrote down the license plate. "I bet if we check that, it'll be the foreman's."

"I wouldn't be at all surprised. We should check the cameras to see when he came in."

"You didn't see him earlier?" Johan asked Galen.

"There was no sign of him coming in, but I think he went through the shipping area. There's a door to the outside right there." He pulled the vehicle up on the side so they could see it.

Johan nodded and continued the theory. "So he parks here, uses that door to enter, and it's just his little secret area. I'll bet he's not even been in the rest of the building in the last ten years."

"I'd agree with you there," Galen said. "Why would he? When you think about it, if you work in this area, do you have any reason to go anywhere else?"

"Not only no reason but probably no will. Guys like that want nothing to do with management and stick to their own areas."

After the slow pass around the parking lot, they left with a wave at the officers standing outside on duty and headed back into town. "She's only a few blocks from here," Galen said. "I didn't realize it was that close."

"Walking distance for sure," Johan said.

"Well, if she needs to save money, she could park her vehicle, I suppose."

"But she still needs the car to get groceries, so it'll save a little on gas but not on insurance."

After that, they pulled up in front of the apartment and stopped. Both looked around, just to see if they'd been followed or to find anything of interest.

"With Edward stepping in with that compliance request,

no one should know that Joy found the missing ketamine, much less reported it to the authorities, right? So do you really think she's in any danger?" Galen asked, as he slowly hopped out. "Seems to me that, chances are, she's a minor cog in this wheel."

"Yeah, but Chelsea got taken out. And was only here three months. With Joy finding something in her first six weeks, that makes her more of a disruption, in my estimation."

Galen nodded, staring at Johan all the while.

"Plus the stakes just went up now, with the CEO being killed," Johan said. "So take out the big cheese at the top and then you don't have to worry about the little guys, or maybe the killer is just working his way down the list, taking them all out who might pose a problem for him."

"When you've already killed one person," Galen said, "everybody else is that much easier. Now he's committed. So, if anybody else is on his list, who he feels needs to go in order to give himself a clean sweep, then he's just getting started."

Johan nodded and headed up the sidewalk toward the front door of the apartment building. As he stopped and turned around, a large truck came barreling down, turning onto the street. He watched from the stoop right at the entrance as it came past his vehicle and slowed. It didn't park, but it went on, as if looking for the right apartment. As it drove past, Johan stared directly into the passenger's face. He frowned, and the vehicle immediately picked up speed and jolted forward.

"Who was that?" Galen asked.

"I'm not sure," Johan said. "Slightly familiar. Tall and slim. I'm thinking male. Maybe somebody from the job, I presume."

"I didn't see a license plate or the driver, but I've got a picture of the truck," Galen said, flicking through his phone. "If somebody works at Westgroup and owns this vehicle, then we would have a connection. But could just as easily have been a friend or family member of someone on staff."

Johan said, "It's almost guaranteed the only reason for coming down here is—"

"There could be lots of reasons," Galen interrupted. "But the prime one, given our circumstances, is to find out if Joy's living here."

"Find out if she's living here and to check out the area."

"All that's changed now that we've been seen."

"Not sure about *we*," Johan said. "Definitely me though."

"Maybe we need to move her out of here," Galen said.

"It's possible," he said. "Or we set the place up as a trap."

"You think they'll be back?"

"Absolutely," he said, as he entered the main hallway and headed for the stairs. "That I can guarantee."

Chapter 11

W HEN A KNOCK came at the door, Tyson hopped up and opened it, getting there just ahead of Joy. She looked at him in surprise as he smiled and said, "It's safer this way."

Uncertain, she stepped back as the knock came again. He opened the door. "About time you got here."

Johan smiled and said, "Right. It's been a bit of a long day at the office." His gaze immediately zoomed in on her.

She could feel the same tingling awareness from the minute the door opened to reveal him there. And the fact that he was looking at her the way he was, well, just sent her stomach churning again, not to mention adding heat to the fire that never seemed to go out down below, not since that damn kiss. She'd been kissed a lot; she'd had multiple boyfriends after all, but there'd been just something behind the punch that he'd packed that made her stop in shock. And she'd felt a response that she had never felt before. She was curious and wanted to know where it would go but not under these circumstances. And she wasn't at all sure she wanted to get hooked up with anybody in Levi's group. Not that she had anything against them, but she had certainly heard enough about them from Kai that Joy knew these were not guys to fool around with, not guys to expect one-night-stand kind of relationships. All good things, but that didn't make her feel any better. She wasn't sure she was at all prepared for this guy.

She smiled at him, but her smile faded when he walked forward, snagged her into his arms, and gave her a big hug.

"*Oof*," she managed.

He set her back down again. "Sorry, there's something very disturbing about seeing your boss on the floor," he muttered. "All I could think of was it could have been you."

She hugged him back at that point because she really hadn't considered that. "It's hard to imagine that he's been shot," she said. "I was just talking to him."

"And we don't know what triggered this," he said, "but you have to stay safe."

"I'm planning on it," she said. To keep herself busy and to avoid the awkward moment of separating, she immediately walked into the kitchen and put on coffee. She could hear the others discussing their day, but there wasn't anything solid, as far as she could tell.

"What now?" she asked when she turned back to face him.

"Dinner," he said promptly. "We didn't have any lunch."

"Ah," she said nodding. "Are we going out then?"

"Or we can bring in," he said. "Either way, your choice."

"Despite my healthy appetite, apparently I don't eat anywhere near the amount that you guys do," she said, "so hardly my choice."

"Good point," Kai said. She looked at the others. "Are we doing any nighttime activities?"

"Possibly," Tyson said, "but it'll be hours yet before the police are done."

"Oh, wow," Joy said. "Maybe I missed something in the

conversation. What are you talking about?"

"We're talking about doing a thorough search of Barlow's office and his house," Johan said.

"Are you allowed to?"

"Technically, no," he said, "which is why we have to wait for the police to finish first."

"And, of course, they'll have taken any forensic evidence they can find."

"True enough," Tyson chimed in. "He does have security in his home though," he said. "I've had that on since I hacked into it this morning, and, so far, nobody's been there."

"Not even the cops?" Johan asked.

"Not yet, no."

"Does he live alone?"

"Yes," Tyson said, "or at least he's been living alone in recent history. The property is in his name only too. Doesn't mean he doesn't have a girlfriend who comes and goes though."

"Or a boyfriend," Kai said. "He broke up with Phyllis for a reason, but we never did hear why, did we?"

"No," Joy said. "I was wondering about doing some research into the news to see if there was anything back then."

"Chances are he hushed it up pretty quickly," Tyson said. "I did do a general search but haven't come up with anything."

"Maybe we need to talk to Phyllis again," Johan said.

"Have you talked to her yet?"

He looked at her, smiled, and nodded. "Just with you there. And when I said *we*, I meant you."

She wrinkled up her nose at him. "I'm not sure she'll want to talk to me after this."

"Do you think she was still holding a torch for your boss?"

"Like I said, a love-hate relationship. I'm sure there were times when she missed him terribly. But I think there were also times when she hated his guts."

"And that can lead to all kinds of behavior."

"True, but I doubt that she killed him."

"Maybe not. It's hard to say at this point in time."

"So, dinner?" Joy looked at the clock. "It's five o'clock."

"You want to get out of here for a bit?" Johan asked her.

"I wouldn't mind, yes," she said. "But obviously it needs to be good food and lots of it, if we're going out for nighttime activities," she said. "And we need to not be too late with dinner."

"No 'we' about it," he said. "You're staying here. And we won't go until after midnight anyway."

She glared at him. "Why can't I go?"

"Because," he said, "it's not what you do."

"Maybe it's what I want to do," she challenged. But really she had no intention of going into Barlow's office or his house in the middle of the night, and the last thing she wanted to do was get caught doing such a thing.

He gave her a big but sweet smile. "Frustration can manifest itself in many ways," he said. "And you'll have to find another way to release it because you're not coming with us." And his word was final.

Her shoulders sagged. She glared at him, her gaze sweeping the three men, who completely ignored her, and Kai just sent her a commiserating look. "Are you going too?"

Kai shook her head. "No, I'm staying here with you."

Joy nodded. "And Tyson?"

"I'm staying here," Tyson said.

"Is that because you're off duty or because you're on duty looking after me?"

He looked up with a gentle smile. "Because I want to spend time with Kai."

And Joy's heart melted a little more. "Okay, you're forgiven."

He grinned. "Thanks for the pass."

Johan glared at her. "So I'm not forgiven when I'm looking into the case that you brought to everybody's attention?"

She glared at him. "That doesn't sound fair either."

"Whatever," he said. "We do what we feel is right, and this is next on our docket."

"Fine."

After that, the discussion turned to dinner. She quickly grabbed her sweater as they swept out of her apartment. She stopped and watched as Johan did something at the door. She looked at him and frowned, a question in her expression.

"Somebody put those bugs in," he said, "and we'll want to know if anybody's been here while we're out."

"Okay," she said, seeing he had just jammed a tiny hair into the door. "What'll that tell you?"

"It'll tell me if somebody opened the door," he explained.

"Can't it fall accidentally?"

"No," he said, "it's wedged in just enough."

With that, he reached out, cupped her elbow, hooked her arm within his, and said, "I hear you were going to cheat me on a steak earlier."

"I was not," she protested, "but I didn't really think about how much you guys eat."

"I'm not a big eater," he said, "but I am somebody who likes to have enough to feel full."

"Which is why we're going out for dinner," she said, "because apparently I can't judge food that well. Or know that a barbecue grill is required."

"It's not a matter of judging food. It's just making sure there's lots of it," he said with a laugh.

At that, she nodded, and, with a final last glance behind her, she headed out to the vehicles. She stopped as she was led to the vehicle that he'd driven. "What if I want to go with Kai?"

"Too bad," he said, "Galen's going with Kai."

"What if I don't want to spend time with you privately?"

"Don't you?" he asked, a suspicion of a smile in his voice.

"Maybe not," she muttered. "You're way too sure of yourself."

He'd turned on the engine but stopped and turned to look at her. "Where you're concerned, I'm not."

She gave him a quick frown at that. "Why not?" she challenged.

"Not sure," he said. "That kiss packed a punch I wasn't expecting."

"Good," she said. "It's only fair that you should have been rattled by it too."

"Meaning, you were as well?"

"You know I was," she said. "I also wasn't expecting that."

"Neither was I," he said. "But it seemed like the right thing to do at the time."

She didn't know what to say about that. She settled back into the seat, frowning. "Where are we going?"

"A large buffet downtown," he said. "I can get two steaks there, if I want them."

"Do you really need two steaks?"

"Not sure," he said with a grin. "Maybe just one will do, depending on whatever else is on tap."

She didn't know what to say to that. There was just something almost surreal about the evening.

"Are you okay?" he asked.

After a few minutes of silence, she nodded. "Yes," she said, "just mellow."

"Good," he said. "It'll be fine, you know?"

She looked at him, hating to hear the insecurity in her voice when she asked, "Are you sure?"

As they came up to a stoplight, he reached across, grabbed her hand, and gently squeezed. "I'll do everything I can to keep you safe."

"I just don't understand why I should be in danger at all," she said.

"Maybe you aren't," he said. The light turned green, and they surged forward again. "Chances are, somebody found out we were there looking into the company, and it spooked them."

"Well, two investigators will do that," she joked.

"But unless they had some reason to think they would be found out, there wouldn't be any doubt or worry about it. To have taken out the boss means that something has changed within the organization."

"You think the thieves did it?"

"It makes sense," he said. "For there to be a large theft ring within the company and *not* associated with the murder stretches the imagination. Generally, if there's a bad element, it's all connected."

"Maybe," she said. "I keep thinking about Chelsea and why anybody would want to kill her."

"And again, if it's connected, it's likely because of what she might have found."

"Nobody even talks about her," she said. "That's really sad. The woman lived and worked there, so you'd think that somebody would have something to say."

"Sure," he said. "So think about yourself and who you've spoken to since you've been there."

She nodded. "Other than the bosses, when asked, nobody. Absolutely nobody."

"Just Phyllis and the other woman, Doris."

"Yes, just those two and then only because we shared that tiny space in the dungeon. But, even then, not much was said and never about anything that mattered."

"Exactly," he said. "That's what it'll be like for a lot of people."

"Kind of depressing though," she said. "Since I've come here, it's been very hard to meet people."

"And that's to be expected in some ways," he said. "I think it's much harder nowadays to meet people, especially if you're not online all the time. Instead people tend to choose one of the many dating apps to hook up."

"I guess I'm a little old-fashioned that way. I'd prefer to like the guy and to know something about him before I go to bed with him," she said with a smile.

"Good," he said, laughing. "Ditto for me."

"Have you ever used the dating apps?"

"No, I haven't," he said. "I'm so busy with work and traveling, it's never been my thing."

"And yet it would be easy," she said. "While you're in town, you could find somebody to spend time with, whether it becomes an in-bed hookup or not. Seems at least fifty, sixty, or one hundred people—all signed up to these apps—

are within a few blocks."

"You've checked them out?"

"I did," she said. "I tried a couple dates with those online apps back in Boston. You know how they say they use computer algorithms to make a good match? I didn't find that to be true, at least not in my case."

"So you didn't pursue any of them?"

"No. I had coffee with one, lunch with another, and met in the park with the third. But, in all three instances, I didn't want to see any of them a second time."

"Interesting," he said. "Billions of dollars go into sorting out those algorithms too."

"I know, right?" Rolling her eyes, she said, "I figured it had to be my answers to the questions on the survey."

"If you were truthful," he said, "then the answers should have helped."

"I was as truthful as I could be, I thought," she said. "It's always a weird feeling though, filling those things out, because there's no real way to explain anything."

"I haven't filled one out," he said, "so I'm not sure how it works."

"It is completely computerized, and isn't that sad? It's like we've lost the human element," she said.

"Yet I think it's meant to put the human element back into our lives," he said.

They came up to yet another red light, and she stared at it, wondering where the other vehicle went. "I guess so, but it seems sad that we can't meet people through the old methods anymore."

"When was the last time you went to a coffee shop and sat alone? Or went to the library? Or volunteered with a large group someplace where you could have met somebody? Or even gone to a bar and just sat there alone?"

"Never, never, never, and never," she said with a laugh.

"Good point. And, if I'm not meeting people at work, then what am I doing to meet people? Nothing."

"Exactly. Whereas online, you can input your answers, meet up with all kinds of people, and choose to follow through to meet them in person. For an awful lot of people, it seems to be working out."

"Maybe so," she said. "For me, it just seems like something's missing."

"Well, obviously something was missing in those hookups that you've made," he said gently. "That doesn't mean the next one won't be great though."

"I deleted my profile before I moved here," she said abruptly.

He shot her a surprised look. "Why?"

"I don't know," she said. "It just didn't feel right for me."

"And I think that's important too," he said. "You have to do what's right for you."

She settled into her seat, feeling better. "When are you guys going out tonight?"

"I don't know for sure," he said. "We'll make that decision when we get back from dinner." He took the truck around several corners, then pulled into a large parking lot.

As they pulled in, she was surprised to see Tyson's SUV already parked there. "I wondered where they'd gotten to," she said in surprise. "They beat us."

"We weren't far behind them," he said, pulling into a larger spot a little farther down from Tyson's vehicle and parked.

She hopped out, waited for him to come around the

back of the truck, and together they walked over to join the other couple. "I couldn't see you," Joy said to Kai. "I figured you were lost."

"Well, we were a little bit ahead," she said, smiling.

"Interesting. I've never been to this restaurant," she said, looking up at the massive building.

"It's known for its ribs," Tyson said. "And we all figured we could do with a good meal."

She smiled and nodded. "I'm always happy to try new restaurants," Joy said.

They walked in and settled in for what turned out to be two hours of good laughter, good friends, and excellent food. Eventually they headed outside.

"I feel like I'll have to be rolled to the truck, I ate so much," Joy said.

"Well, that's both the good and the bad thing about a buffet," Tyson said, laughing as his arm found its way around Kai.

Mimicking the same movement, Johan stepped up beside Joy, wrapping an arm around her shoulders and tugging her closer. "Besides, if you have to be rolled to the truck," he said, "that would look pretty cute."

"No," she groaned. "Not cute at all." She watched as they separated into the same two vehicles again. He held open the truck door and assisted her up. "How come it's just us two again?"

"Because I arranged it that way," he said with a wicked grin. And then he shut the door, leaving her alone with her thoughts.

JOHAN OPENED THE driver's side door, hopped into his

truck, and smiled at the confused look on her face.

"Are you flirting with me?" Joy demanded.

He laughed out loud. "I can see you're a little out of practice with the social scene."

She rolled her eyes at him. "I know I'm a little slow," she said, "but, if you're arranging all this, at least tell me if it's because you're keeping me safe or because you're interested in me."

"Both, I would say. I really like you. And there are definitely sparks between us."

"That's just physical," she said, as she stared out the window.

"And physical is a great start to a relationship."

"No," she said. "It's a great add-on to a relationship. But a relationship shouldn't be based *on* the sparks."

"No, maybe not," he said. "But how do you know who to have a relationship with if you can't feel the sparks from the beginning?"

For that, she didn't have any answer.

He finally pulled up in front of her apartment and said, "We'll come up and have coffee before we leave."

"So how do you stop your bladder from running when you're on a job like this?"

Her prosaic comment made him laugh out loud. "We'll be sure to use the bathroom first," he assured her, as she flashed him a grin.

"That's all right," she said. "You stealth types must have all kinds of ways to get around awkward situations."

"Well, you'd think so," he said, "but sometimes I wonder."

"Oh, I see you're human too, huh?"

"Yeah. Sure I am, and bodily functions are not always

the most amiable," he said with a smile, as he parked and shut off the engine. He came around to her side to help her out.

At that point, she noted he'd parked a block away. "Is there another reason you have for doing this?"

"I don't want to be too close and don't necessarily want them to see us directly entering the building. And, if we have to leave, we don't want people easily watching both vehicles."

"Got it," she said. "Is it okay if we walk up to the apartment together?"

"Absolutely," he said with a smile. He reached out a hand, and she placed hers in it; then together they walked the block back to her place.

"This feels very date-like," she said, her words echoing her earlier thoughts.

"Good," he said, "then consider it our first date."

"Will there be a second one?"

"Yes," he said smoothly. Not wanting to give her any chance to think that it was anything other than a date, he said, "When this nightmare is over, I'd love to spend more time with you."

"Kai suggested I move to the suburbs so she and I could be closer and could spend more time together," she said.

"That would be a great idea," he said, "but do you want to move?"

"I don't want to stay where the bugs were found, that's for sure." She shrugged. "But moving? I'm not particularly interested in that, but mostly because I don't want to go through the physical effort again."

"Did you have a reason for being here in downtown Houston?"

"No, not really. I was looking at Dallas versus Houston and ended up with Houston, though it was pretty arbitrary, if for no other reason than to be closer to Kai."

"You'd also be closer to me," he said.

"How long are you staying in the US though? I thought you were from Africa?"

"My stay is open-ended," he said. "I'm an American citizen, so I can come and go as I want."

"Moving here was a fast decision for me," she said, "and I didn't really care either way at the time."

"You don't appear to have much stuff."

"No, I don't," she said. "Less than you think, because I rented the apartment furnished."

As they walked, he paused for a moment and turned to look at her. "Really?"

She shrugged. "I just came with what I could fit in my car."

"Well, that makes it easier, as long as you don't have a long lease."

"No, I'm month-to-month. I'll have to pay for another month obviously, if I give notice, but there's nothing else keeping me here, except for my job, and you've seen how that's going."

"There could be heavy fallout after the media gets hold of the news about Barlow."

"I was checking to see if they had already gotten it, but, so far, there's been no announcement."

"I was checking too," he said. "I'm surprised at that. But it is the weekend, and sometimes the news is a bit behind on business things like this."

"Most of the time it seems like they're right there on the spot," she said.

"I'm sure it'll be out tomorrow."

They walked comfortably together, their fingers linked.

He thought about her moving closer to him and Kai and really liked the idea. "We could see a lot more of each other if you moved closer to the compound," he said suddenly.

"We could," she said, "but I don't want to make a move based on that potential," she said. "I have to be happy in Houston's outskirts, even if we don't spend any more time together. The Houston area is potentially only a short-term answer for you too."

They had reached the main entrance to her building. He opened the door and let her in first. "You're right." He nodded. "Pick a spot where you want to live," he said. "And, if we choose to, we'll make it happen."

"True," she said with a bright smile. "I'm still not sure exactly how this is happening though."

"Well, I could admit that I saw something I liked, and I wanted it, so I went after it."

"And yet you said yourself that you were surprised by the kiss."

"I was," he said. "Delightfully surprised. But I was also surprised at the instinct to kiss you because it was not planned." They walked down the main hallway toward the elevators.

"Well, that makes me feel better," she said with a smile. "I didn't really want to be targeted."

"Never targeted," he assured her. He tugged her into his arms. "We could repeat the kiss just to make sure it was the real thing."

She smiled up at him, looped her arms around his neck, and whispered, "Well, we could," she said, "particularly if nobody will see us."

"The hallway's empty right now." He lowered his head and kissed her thoroughly. She responded, feeling the exact same surge of passion that had happened before. When they broke apart, their chests were heaving, and her breasts were heavy.

"Well," she said, "we definitely need to dole that out in small doses."

He hit the button for the elevator. "True enough," he agreed, as he snatched her hand and walked her inside the elevator. "Either that or we need to set aside some scheduled time and let the inferno blaze away."

She smiled as they exited the elevator and walked to her apartment. "I might be up for that too," she said, "but not until this mess is over with."

He smiled, dropped down to check the hair he'd left in the door, and froze. "Well, you won't be away from me for any time in the near future," he said, "because that hair is gone."

Chapter 12

J OY STARED DOWN at him in horror. He held up a finger
to his lips. "We don't know if they're inside or not," he
whispered as he stood.

She shook her head in disbelief. "Couldn't he have come
and gone? Couldn't that be just because the others are ahead
of us?"

He shook his head. "They aren't ahead of us," he said.
"They're behind us."

She frowned. "No," she said, "they left before us."

"Yes, but I took a shortcut," he explained.

Just behind them the elevator doors opened, and the
other three walked out, talking. When they saw them, Kai
raised her hand, preparing to call out.

Johan immediately held up a hand and pointed at the
door. Silence ensued as the others strode toward them. It
wasn't lost on Joy that Kai immediately complied with the
unspoken signal without argument or question.

"Let's go in first," Galen whispered to Johan.

Gently motioning Joy back toward Tyson and Kai, Johan then crouched on one side of the door, with Galen
crouched on the other. On the count of three they burst
inside.

She watched in disbelief because the door should have
been locked, but it wasn't. Or it popped underneath their

efforts. They made it look like opening a child's toy. They went in, and there was absolute silence.

She stared at Kai and whispered, "Is it good or bad?"

Her face was grim, but she answered, "It's too early to tell."

Tyson stepped up, so that he stood in front of both women, and whispered, "They haven't called out all clear," he said, "so that's not a good sign."

Joy nodded slowly. "Right. In other words, somebody could be in there, and now they're holding Galen and Johan captive."

Tyson looked at her, surprised, one eyebrow raised. "Or not."

She glared at him, understanding that all these macho guys probably had skills well beyond anything she'd ever seen before, but they could still be taken down by guns with silencers or men with better skills and better weapons. She'd just seen the two guys pull handguns from somewhere, which blew her away, since she hadn't even realized either of them were carrying. But suddenly they had guns in their hands, and they popped through the door. But then, this was Texas, and a lot of people were armed that she wasn't really aware of. It was something she might even want to look at moving forward. She shook her head at that. "This is unbelievable," she whispered.

"Now it confirms what we're afraid of," Tyson said.

She glared at his back. "I still don't want anything to do with it."

"Too late," Kai said, as she reached over to touch Joy's fingers with her own. "Trust your team."

Joy squeezed her friend's hand. "I do trust them," she said, "but this is just so far beyond anything I'm used to."

Just then they heard a shout. "Clear!"

Tyson walked forward with one of the women on either side. At the doorway they stopped. Johan stood just a few feet in, his hands on his hips, surveying her apartment.

She took a step toward the inside, then stopped and cried out in horror. "Oh, my God," she said. "What did they do?" Every piece of furniture had been upended and trashed. The seat cushions were ripped open, so stuffing was everywhere. On the back of the couch a big gash ran from one side to the other, so there was absolutely no way to fix it beyond reupholstering the whole thing. The carpet had something spread on top of it. She wasn't exactly sure what it was, but it looked like it could have been eggs.

She started to walk into the living room, but Johan reached out a hand to stop her. And then she saw the rest of the room, on the opposite side of the couch. High on the wall in some red spray paint was the word *bitch*, and just below that was *snitch*, and still below that was *liar*, then below that was *dead*.

She swallowed hard, her hand going to her mouth as she stared in horror at what somebody had done to her life. She could feel the tears gathering in the corners of her eyes. Tears she was desperate not to shed, but there was absolutely no holding them back. They leaked slowly down her cheeks, until Johan gave a muffled exclamation and pulled her into his arms. She stood here, shaking in his grasp, as she looked around. "Why?" she whispered.

"You know why," he said. "This is to scare you. It's a warning."

"The last word means it's a threat," Kai said, stepping up behind them. "It may have started off as a rampage or as a warning for her to get the hell out of here, but the last line has a much more ominous tone."

Joy agreed that, if they'd left it at just calling her a liar, she wouldn't have considered her life so much in danger, but, by adding *dead*, that upped the ante completely. She didn't even know how to react, what to say, or what to think. She turned to look in the direction of her bedroom. "Do I even want to go in there?"

Johan shook his head. "You won't like anything about it," he said. "It's like this, only worse."

She reached up, grabbed his shirt, and squeezed it as hard as she could while he just held her close. "How could it be any worse?"

"Listen. It'll be fine," he said.

She reared back and glared at him. "How could any of this be fine?" she said. "This is so far from fine that it's not funny."

"That's true," he said. "But it is what it is, and we'll deal with that. Let's look at your bedroom and see if there's anything salvageable."

Swallowing hard, she walked down the short hallway to her bedroom with Johan at her side. She stared, mute at the devastation in her room. "What did they do? Save the worst for here?" she asked sarcastically.

"Well, this makes it more personal, doesn't it?" he said. "It's not only your room, it's your bed. It's where you sleep, where you're secure at night. Or should be."

She swallowed, half understanding what he said, yet not wanting to delve any deeper into it. "I suppose," she whispered, "but it still sucks."

"Yes, it does," he said, his arm coming around her shoulders to tuck her up a little closer yet again. "It definitely does."

Not only had the bed been slashed but the headboard, the mattress, and everything in the closet. Then it was all piled on the floor and covered in even more spray paint. She just stared, unable to process the enormity of what she saw.

Kai stepped forward and said, "Let's see if we can salvage anything out of this," she said, "and then we'll get you out of here."

"Why?" she asked, her tone flat. "What else can anybody do to me?"

"You don't want to hear the answer to that," Johan said. "And you're in shock right now, so I suggest you sit down in the kitchen, and I can go through this stuff with Kai."

But she took a deep breath, shook her head, and said, "Luckily anything of a sentimental value that I sold when I downsized for this move, I took pictures of. So all my family pictures and the memories are in the cloud. Still, I need to settle down, get my wits back. I need to see the area to remind me what I would want most to save from here. So you won't know what it is. I don't yet know what it is. Just give me a minute."

"You don't have a whole lot here, right?"

"I came with what would fit in my car. Remember?" she said. "Everything else in here belongs to the apartment owner."

"So you sublet it?"

"Yes," she said quietly, "and, man, he won't be happy."

"Maybe not," Tyson said. "But we can contact him and he should have insurance."

"Do we need to call the cops?"

"They've already been called," Galen said, holding up his phone. "They'll be here in about ten to fifteen minutes, so, if you want something, you better get it now."

She didn't quite understand why it was important until Johan nudged her gently back around to face the room, saying, "Once the cops are here, and they make the connection to the murder scene at work, and they'll bring in forensics, and they'll be here for hours and hours going through stuff, and you may not get anything back because it may all be held as evidence."

"On that note," Kai said, "let me take a bunch of photos of the place."

Joy stepped forward carefully, realizing every one of her drawers had been upended. "I don't even know if there's anything salvageable. Whoever did this must have left here covered in paint." She motioned toward a pile of clothing that had been sprayed on the top and on bottom. Obviously whoever did this had kicked over the pile just to coat both sides. She peered into the closet, but they had taken everything out. She stood here, absolutely stunned. She looked up at him. "Find my laptop, will you?"

"Where did you keep it?"

Joy looked over at Kai. "Do you remember where I had it before we left?"

"You didn't have it out with us," Tyson said, "and we took all our gear back to the vehicle when we left."

She looked at him, frowning. "Were you expecting this?"

"We've come to learn the hard way that, even when we don't expect this," he said with a wave of his hand, "we expect something."

"Well, I had a laptop. I usually kept it in the night table in the bottom drawer," she said.

Johan made his way over to the night table, which had been dumped upside down. He lifted it up, and there was her laptop. She cried out in joy as he grabbed it and handed it to her. "Wait. Let me get these cables."

She nodded and pointed to the charger. "Yes, please, both chargers. One's for my cell phone, and the other is for my laptop."

As he gave them to her, he noticed a copy of a popular graphic novel had come out of the nightstand, so he picked that up too. Then she slowly retreated, trying to figure out if she even wanted anything else here.

Kai reached out for a bra but stopped midway as it was covered in paint. A stack of panties was off to the side, but they had been painted too all over. "Several paint cans were used here," Kai said. "I don't think you'll want anything here."

Joy shook her head. "Not really. I've got my laptop and phone, and I guess everything else is replaceable." But her voice dropped as she realized the enormity of the cost to replace everything.

"Do you have renter's insurance?" Tyson asked behind her.

She stared at him, realizing what he meant. "No," she whispered. "I don't. If I'm liable for all this, I'm really screwed."

"You won't be liable for it," Kai said, "but it would help if you could get a few hundred dollars to replace some of this." And she waved her hand at the clothing.

"That'll take more than a few hundred dollars," Joy said sadly. "I don't spend much on clothes, but, to replace it all at once, well, it'll be a few thousand for sure."

"You brought some winter clothes with you too, I see," Tyson said, motioning to the closet where coats had been dumped on the floor and spray-painted on top.

"I did a huge cleanup before I left Boston," she whispered. "This is what I decided to keep because it seemed better suited for here. I was going to buy more clothes later, figuring Texas malls would have better options for the temperate weather here."

"Did you buy more once you got here?"

She shook her head. "I didn't get a chance yet," she said. "I was just making do with my old clothes, trying to get a few more paychecks behind me."

"Well, guess what?" Johan said. "I don't think you can wait any longer."

JOHAN HADN'T WANTED to be brutal in his tone, but she could do only so much standing here. She groaned and turned away, walking into the kitchen. She checked in a few of the cupboards, found a bit of food, then opened the fridge. There she cried out because the milk had been poured out on the inside, and the eggs had been smashed. She'd just picked up extra groceries with Kai, and the steaks were long gone, as they'd been torn out of their containers, soaked in milk, and tossed on the lower shelves of the fridge.

She slowly closed the fridge and turned to look at Johan. "What am I supposed to do now?"

The bewilderment in her voice got to him the most. "Well, first off," he said, "we have a hotel suite, so you can come stay with us. Kai and Tyson can grab a hotel room there as well," he said. "The police will be here soon, and it depends on what they say, but no way you can stay here obviously."

"Why are you both in a hotel, when I thought the compound was nearby, just on the outskirts of Houston?" Joy asked.

With a nod to Kai, Johan explained. "Kai and Ice both wanted us closer to you, considering the ketamine angle. Which has proved to be a good instinct, what with the threats to you and the murder of Barlow, plus finding out Chelsea may have been murdered as well."

She looked down at her watch. "It's Saturday, and I suppose it's too late to shop, isn't it?"

"No, depending on how long the cops keep us here," Kai said. "The malls will be open until nine o'clock. You and I can hopefully go out and at least get you a couple outfits. If nothing else, some underclothes and a few pairs of leggings and shirts that you can wear to work."

"Okay," she said, staring down at her only a pair of jeans. "Of course I'm wearing jeans, the one thing I can't wear to work."

"Maybe," Kai said. "But they sure look good on you, and they're new, so better that they destroyed some older stuff, and you've got the new pair."

She nodded slowly and took several steps back.

When a hard knock sounded on the door, she cried out. Johan immediately reached out to calm her down. "It's all right," he said.

She shook her head. "You keep saying that." She watched as Galen opened the door to see the manager there with several cops.

They stepped inside, and the manager cried out, "Good Lord," he snapped. "Who did this?"

"Well, if you had any security cameras in the building," Tyson said in a mild tone, "we might be able to find out."

The cops turned to look at the manager, who shrugged. "No, there are no security cameras here."

The cops took one look around, one of them shoving his

hat back off his forehead to scratch at the hair underneath. "Somebody took their time here."

"But they didn't have a whole lot of time," Joy said. "We were only gone a couple hours for dinner."

"Got it," he said, and he proceeded to take information from all of them.

Johan stayed close to Joy the whole time. He could see her starting to flag. Her energy level was going down, and her will to respond civilly was failing as well. But it was what it was, and he would just be sure he was here for her as much as he could be. In the back of his mind though, he knew that the time frame had just been accelerated. Even now they would be under watch. Somebody was out there enjoying the show. Johan just wanted to make sure they didn't get to see too much more.

Chapter 13

J OY WOKE UP the next morning in a hotel room all alone, feeling incredibly tired, worn out, and sad. The things that people did to each other were just so depressing. She didn't deserve what these assholes had done to her. She didn't have much money. Only her fourth paycheck was coming in now, and that wasn't enough to recoup the cost of her move to a new apartment, her new clothes, and one month's notice at her current apartment building, all especially if she lost her job too. She'd hit her savings pretty hard for the months that she didn't have any money coming in. And now she was out the rent as well.

That was beyond disturbing because she still had to come up with the money to stay somewhere else. At the moment she was in the same hotel as the others. Kai and Tyson had taken a room beside them, and Joy was in a room between the two groups. At least she was alone, though that was both good and bad.

Part of her was sad, and another part of her was over-joyed. Nothing like a quiet space to sort herself out. She was also terribly lonely. Somebody out there had targeted her, and she didn't know who, but she felt that sense of being victimized. She knew it was a sad state of affairs for her to feel like that, but it also went along with everything else that was happening. Would she have still gone through with this if she'd realized how personally involved she would end up being? She knew the answer should be yes, but she was still too confused to sort herself out.

When a knock came at the door, she froze and then forced herself to relax. "Who is it?"

"It's Johan," he called through the door.

She hopped up, wrapped the hotel room robe around her, and opened the door. He carried a tray of coffee. She smiled and let him in. "Because you've got the coffee," she announced, "I'm happy to have you come in."

He smiled and set it down, then looked at her in concern. "Did you get any sleep?"

"Maybe, the jury is out as to whether it was a good sleep though," she said. "It was a pretty late night before we finally got in here."

"It was," he said. "Well after midnight, as I recall."

"Well, it put a stop to you going out and getting into trouble, so maybe that was a good thing."

He smiled. "I'm just heading out now with Galen."

"What time is it?"

"It's only seven o'clock," he said.

"Then how did you know I was awake?" she protested.

"I figured, if you were sound asleep, you wouldn't have answered the door," he said.

She frowned up at him, not sure she wanted to believe his logic. But she crawled back into bed, pulled the covers to her waist, and he handed her a cup of coffee. "You sure you want to go now?" she asked. "There is no darkness to hide your movements."

"It's not darkness we need," he said. "I'm a big believer and feel like, when the time was right, things would happen on their own."

She laughed at that. "If you say so. Doesn't say much for my current situation, does it?" She waved him off. "Thanks for the coffee delivery."

He pointed to the carafe and said, "There's more, if you want it."

She nodded. "Please stay in touch. I don't want to be sitting here, wondering what I'm supposed to do at checkout time."

"We're here for at least tonight," he said.

She frowned up at him. "That's expensive."

"That's not your problem right now," he said. "We have bigger issues."

She snorted at that, but he was soon gone. She tried not to worry about the cost of the hotel, but she had few options right now. Almost immediately another knock came at her door.

After looking through the peephole, she opened the door and said, "Come on in."

Kai poked her head in, saw the coffee, and grinned. "Here I was going to offer you coffee," she said, "but Johan beat me to it. I should have known."

There was just something so teasing about her voice that Joy could feel the heat washing up her cheeks. "Well, I slept alone," she said, "so obviously there isn't anything going on between us."

"Oh, he would have stayed with you, if you've given him a chance," she said. "But he was more concerned about you getting a good night's sleep after last night than anything else."

"Well, I did get some," she said, relaxing against the headboard, taking a sip of her coffee. "It's just so unbelievable, and I have so much now to deal with that I don't even know how to start."

"Right," she said, "and that's something we can sort out right now." She pulled up a chair, sat down beside Joy, putting her feet up on the bed.

"Don't you want coffee?" Joy pointed at the carafe. "More is in that, and an extra cup is nearby."

Kai nodded, hopped to her feet, went to the tray, and poured herself a cup. She came back with the pot and topped off Joy's cup while she was at it. "Let's make a list," she said, "and see what we need to do first."

"Well, seeing how we didn't go to the mall last night," Joy joked, "I need to shower, get dressed in the same dirty clothes, then find new clothes."

"Malls don't open until at least nine o'clock here," she said, "so we'll have breakfast first."

The two women put their heads together, focused on the list, and jotted down things she needed to get. "What about your IDs?"

"In my purse," she said. "I don't really have much else."

"Passport?"

"I just applied for one," she said. "I don't have it yet."

"Well, that's good," she said. "So you've got your laptop, your phone, your purse, all your credit cards, and stuff like that. So you really just need clothing and personal items, right?"

"Right," she said. "Especially considering I couldn't even brush my teeth last night or this morning."

Kai looked up and nodded in understanding. "So we need to hit a drugstore and a place to buy clothing."

"What's Tyson going to do while we're roaming around in the malls?" she joked. "I highly doubt he wants to come with us."

Kai smiled. "Tyson went with the guys."

WITH THE THREE of them on different corners of the property, Johan left the other two outside and approached Barlow's house from the back. He'd already done a quick reconnaissance earlier and knew this was the best entrance. He made his way inside the house, popping the lock easily.

It was early morning, and nobody was out and about. It was a Sunday, so most people were asleep, but he could never assume that he hadn't been seen, so he walked calmly and naturally, as if he were expected to be here.

Johan pulled on disposable gloves. Inside the house was nothing but silence. The man Barlow had lived alone per their research. He'd had a series of girlfriends, but apparently nothing lasting since Phyllis, which was close to twenty-four years ago now by Johan's preliminary research. He quickly searched the main floor, went downstairs, but it was just a basement, empty except for weight equipment gathering dust in a corner. The other side held a kayak and a canoe, both shiny and clean, yet dusty. As if never used. He made his way now to the second floor. The spare room was empty but laid out in case somebody wanted to stay, including a robe across the bed. He frowned at that and stepped into the bathroom, wondering if that was the way he treated all his visitors or if somebody had been here recently. But the bathroom was completely clean, with no sign of water in the tub or shower. It looked like that's how he left it for guests.

Heading into the master bedroom, he stopped to study the layout. A huge round bed was the centerpiece, so the guy had probably thought he was some kind of Don Juan. Even had thick red velvet bedding on top. Johan winced at the garishness of it all. "Hope that worked for you, buddy," he muttered.

But considering Barlow hadn't had a steady relationship in a long time, Johan didn't think it could have. He wandered around the room, checking behind the pictures on the wall. He opened the dressers, seeing nothing but standard clothing and things he would expect to see in anybody's room. In the closets were multiple suits, all high-end yet flashy, and almost as if someone had put every item of one outfit up together. The ties and shirts were with the suits, as if Barlow took everything off the hanger and got dressed, then put it in the laundry, and it all came back that way.

This bathroom looked a little more lived-in than the other one. Johan found shaving gear, some over-the-counter medication for headaches on a side counter, shampoo in the shower, toilet paper on the roll, and more stacked up behind it. So this was the bathroom that Barlow used the most.

Johan headed to the night table on what would be the spare side first and found it empty. He walked over to the other side, the one Barlow should have been using all the time, and found it empty as well. That surprised Johan. Where was his laptop? Where was Barlow's e-reader? Where was the phone, the chargers, the simple things in life that made all the electronics work these days? It made no sense to have none of that here, unless there was another place he stored his electronics, or if somebody had come through and taken it all. Johan sent a quick message to Ice. Her response made the most sense. The cops had picked up the electronics.

He turned his attention to the bed, lifting the pillows. Then, on a whim, he flipped off the bedding, so he could see the sides of the mattresses, and then, on his knees, checked under the bed. Nothing. He lifted the top mattress, lifted the box spring, and bingo, an envelope was taped underneath.

He quickly detached the envelope, put the bed back together, so it looked the way it should, then headed back out to look for any electronics. But he couldn't find anything.

Finally, back in the home office, where Barlow should have had a laptop on his desk, Johan stopped and looked at all the big portraits and heavy paintings on the walls. He quickly lifted several of them, looking for a safe, and found it in the wall behind the office desk. He removed the painting, standing it up on the floor, then quickly texted the two men outside about what he'd found. Even though he hadn't had a chance to open the envelope yet, he wanted to try to crack the safe first.

Tyson texted back. **I'm coming in. Galen will stay on guard.**

Johan waited for Tyson to show up, pointing out the safe. Tyson's eyebrows shot up, his hands already in gloves too. "That's relatively new," he said, rubbing his hands together.

"So, does that mean you want to take a crack at it first?"

"Oh, I so do," Tyson said with a big grin. "May I?"

"Go for it," Johan said. "I'll go through this envelope while you do that. By the way, the cops have collected all the electronics."

While Tyson worked on the safe, Johan turned and opened the envelope. What he pulled out made him whistle in surprise.

Distracted, Tyson turned, just in time to see photos of several men in tight grips, obviously making love. These were deeply sexual images in black and white. "Blackmail?" Tyson asked.

"Maybe," Johan said. "Nothing else in here but the photos."

"And they were taped under the bed?"

"Yes," Johan said. "Not easily accessible but hidden for safekeeping."

"Maybe you better turn this place over a little bit further and see if anything else like that is hanging around."

"My vote is to check inside the safe first," Johan said.

Just then, Tyson's nimble fingers popped the combination lock, and the safe made a distinctive *click*. He reached over, dropped the lever, and opened the safe. Inside were stacks and stacks of money. They both whistled.

"Wow, so he kept a ton of cash on hand. Why?" Johan asked.

"I'm not sure, but maybe some of this will help." Tyson reached forward and pulled out several more envelopes and what looked like jewelry cases. As he opened the jewelry cases, he found very expensive pieces, with emeralds, rubies, and sapphires. Each was in a color-coordinated box, so red for the rubies, the emeralds were in a green box, and the box for the sapphires was blue. He put them back into the safe, and they pulled out a small book and another big envelope. They opened both and took a closer look.

"Same thing but different people in the photos," Johan said.

"Definitely blackmail then," Tyson said.

They spread the pictures out and took careful photographs of every one of them and then put the envelope back in the safe. The little book Johan held out and said, "This looks like his blackmail ledger."

They shook their heads at the initials, but it seemed to be only four guys.

"Two men in each image, but is he blackmailing both of them?" Tyson asked.

"Maybe, but look at these prices. Five thousand a month from each of them, so he's getting twenty grand a month." Johan turned to look at the money in the safe. "You know that's probably what all that cash is."

"And the dates are for the last five years," Tyson said. "I wonder if this is a new venture, or if the other ones just stopped paying?"

"It's hard to say," Johan noted. "Let's take photos of the ledger, jewelry, the stash of cash, and then we'll tell Levi, so that he can nicely give the information to the cops, so they come back and take another look." Johan snorted. "You know what? In Africa the murderer would have taken this money and the jewels after killing Barlow, spoils of war and all that, saving the authorities from all that paperwork."

"But we're not in Africa," Tyson cited. "But it does raise a good point. If the murderer was one of the guys being blackmailed, surely he would want his money back. So why didn't he look for a safe himself?"

Johan nodded. "Maybe he doesn't have your safe-cracking skills." By the time they had taken the needed photographs and had noted the ranges of the consecutive serial numbers on the cash, and then replaced everything in the safe, the two men stood in the front hallway and surveyed the area. "Does it feel like we're missing something?"

"Maybe," Tyson agreed, "but I would suggest it's probably at work, if something is missing."

"Let's go there next then." Quickly Johan texted Galen that they were coming out.

Just as they were about to open the front door, Galen sent a warning. **Somebody just pulled into the driveway. Go out the back.**

Shit," Johan said, as they strode as fast as they could to the kitchen and let themselves out.

With Galen keeping watch, telling them as somebody walked up to the front door with a key, Tyson and Johan were already over the fence and in the neighbor's yard. They quickly regrouped a block away, and then, with Galen driving, they drove past the house so they could look at the vehicle.

"I wonder who that is," Tyson said. Neither of them recognized the vehicle, but they were both busy taking photos of it so they could trace it later.

"No way to know right now," Johan replied. "The thing is, we need a copy of the will or at least to find out who inherits."

"And sometimes it's not always about what somebody'll get," Tyson noted. "It can often be as much about what's going to stop. The lawyers will have a will somewhere. Possibly life insurance too. Ice can look into that."

"Meaning, the blackmail," Johan noted.

"Yes, that's quite possible," Galen said.

"Let's head back to the gals," Tyson said. He checked his phone and snorted. "Apparently they're at the mall."

"Of course they are," Johan said. "Joy doesn't have any clothes."

"They haven't eaten either. They were going to go for brunch first. Shall we meet them?"

"Absolutely." He quickly set up arrangements, and they headed straight to the restaurant.

Soon the two women wandered in, looking around. The men had arrived first and were already seated. Joy looked around and smiled when she saw Johan.

He got up, walked over, and gave her a gentle hug and a kiss on the forehead. "So how are you doing now?"

Chapter 14

J OY WRAPPED AN arm around him, surprised at just how natural it felt. "After the cup of coffee?" she teased. "I feel much better. We went for a long walk because the malls weren't open yet," she said. "Then we were just thinking about stopping for brunch when you guys said you were done."

He nodded and motioned toward the booth they had settled into at the back of the restaurant. They were all alone with nobody around them.

As soon as they were seated, Kai leaned forward expectantly. "And?"

"How do you know there's an 'and' anyway?" Tyson asked.

She smiled. "I can see that you guys found something."

"A safe with some naughty photos and a black book. More naughty photos taped under the bed," he said.

Joy stared at them. "And what difference does that make?"

"The photos were of men with men," Johan said in a low voice. "And I presume that they are of people who don't want anyone to be aware of their sexual proclivities."

"So blackmail?"

He nodded. "That's what we're thinking. But we don't recognize the faces. Can you take a look?" Joy nodded, and he brought up several of the photos and enlarged them so she could see the faces.

She shook her head. "No, I don't know any of these men."

He nodded. "We're sending them to Levi, hoping he can ID them."

"Barlow was well-paid by the company," Joy said. "He wouldn't need to blackmail anybody."

"People blackmail for all kinds of reasons," Kai said gently. "It's not always about money. It's often about revenge. It can be about power plays. Sometimes even for fun."

"You guys don't deal with very nice people," Joy announced.

Tyson chuckled. "No, we don't," he said. "We often see the dregs of the dregs, but that doesn't mean we have to be pulled into it with them."

"No," Kai said. "Taking the high road isn't always that easy though."

"Very true. And Barlow was getting five thousand a month from four different people," Johan said. "A lot of cash was inside that safe."

"What?" Joy cried out. "Five thousand dollars a month? From each?" The three men nodded. She sank back, looked over at Kai, and said, "I'm in the wrong business."

Kai chuckled. "Of course it's lucrative, and, in this case, instead of charging them hundreds of thousands of dollars, he kept bleeding them for a little bit every month, but then it never ends."

"Well, it's ended now," Joy said. "Do you think that's what happened?"

"It's a very viable possibility," Johan said. "That's one of the reasons for sending the information to Levi. Then we can have him contact the detective to say that he 'heard rumors'"—a phrase he put in air quotes—"so they could come and check out the house."

"And, of course, we can't just hand over the information, can we?"

"Not without having interfered with the police investigation," Johan said cheerfully.

Joy rolled her eyes at him. "Which is what you just did."

"I didn't do anything," he said, innocent like.

"If we could identify these men," Joy said, "you'd have four suspects."

"We also don't know if anybody else is being blackmailed," Johan said. "We have four people, but we don't know if it's all four men in these photos or if Barlow has other photos somewhere."

"You mean, like at his office?" Joy said.

"Yeah."

"Any idea how many men are on the board?" Galen asked Joy.

"Not sure," she said. "I'm sure their financial IPOs would tell us."

Tyson was already looking it up. "Looks like six board members."

"And Barlow is one of them?"

He nodded. "So five others."

"One's a woman," Tyson said. "I'm looking for images right now." He whistled silently and then stopped when the waitress came over with a coffeepot and filled everybody's cups and handed out menus. He waited until she was gone, then he brought up a face. As they all looked at it, eyebrows shot up as they recognized the guy from one of the photos.

"Barlow was blackmailing board members?" Kai asked.

"Looks like one at least."

"It depends. Remember. We don't have the photos matched to the notations in the ledger book yet," Johan said.

"Just a second, we'll see who else is on the board." Tyson waited for a photo to load. "So it looks like the two men in the photos under the bed are both board members," he said. "I can't find the other two men."

"That would make Barlow happy, wouldn't it?" Johan said. "He's being chased out of his company, so he gets back at them."

Joy shook her head. "He sits there, day in and day out, knowing that he's the one bleeding them dry. Do you think they knew?"

"Probably not right away," Johan said. "The question is, what changed and how?"

"Well, what changed was me," Joy said, "but I didn't have anything to do with the blackmail."

"No," Kai interrupted, "but I wonder if what you started made him feel like he needed to move something or to change something. What if it made him a little more insecure? Maybe he upped the amounts of the blackmail or something."

"Maybe he didn't change anything," Johan said. "Maybe somehow somebody finally found out what he was doing?"

"Until we know more, it'll be hard to say," Kai said.

"And who was the man who went to the house?" Johan asked.

"Levi's checking the license plate with the DMV," Galen said. "I'm waiting to hear back." Just then his phone buzzed. Snatching it up, he looked and said, "Ricardo Wimberly."

"Any relationship to Barlow?" Tyson asked.

"Well, you would think so, but who knows?" Galen said.

"Let me bring up the image." He brought up the DMV photo, but nobody recognized him from the photo. Galen held it up so they could take a good second look, but everybody shook their heads. Then he stopped. "It's an old ugly photo of the IT guy. And the guy I saw skulking around in the shadows a few days ago."

Joy asked to hold it for a moment. She studied it for a few minutes. "I think you're right," she said. "I think maybe he works in the IT department," she replied, "but I'm not sure about that."

"Well, I can check to see if he works at the company," Tyson said, immediately tapping away on his phone too. "I like that he works in the IT department. Would explain so much. Like the security cards, the hacking, even the inventory numbers ..."

Joy was amazed at how much they could do just while sitting here having coffee.

"Did I hear someone say he had keys to Barlow's house?" Kai asked.

Galen said, "Yeah. That means that he was either a friend, family, or maybe a lover."

"Oh, I hadn't considered that maybe he was gay too," Joy said, and she frowned. "Maybe that's why Barlow doesn't have any long-term relationships?"

"It's possible." Johan looked at Joy. "Maybe that's what broke up him and Phyllis?"

"Maybe," Joy said. "But then I'd really be thinking that she was the one blackmailing him instead."

At that, there was silence, as everybody contemplated what Joy said. They thought about the story Phyllis had told Joy and where Phyllis was currently working.

"You know what? That's not out of the realm of possibility," Johan said. "Any idea what her lifestyle is like?"

"No," Joy said. "She doesn't dress fancy and doesn't wear any accessories that I would consider expensive. I don't know what she drives or where she lives because she's never opened up about it."

"Well, maybe we need to check into her life a little more too," Galen said, his phone out again.

"Look at the three of you," Joy said, laughing. "You're all sitting here on your phones."

"If we were anybody else," Kai said, "I'd give them heck for phones at the table. But in this instance—"

"Exactly," Joy said. "I still can't see how any of this blackmail operation has to do with my apartment being trashed."

"Well," Johan said, "I can't either, but that doesn't mean it doesn't. Something has somebody pissed off at you."

She sank back as she thought about it and nodded. "It just sucks though. It seems like we have all these puzzle pieces, and none of them fit together."

"They will," Johan said with quiet confidence. "They definitely will."

THE GUYS CAME up with all kinds of information, but Phyllis was still a bit of a blank slate. She owned a small Pontiac that was seven years old. She didn't appear to have any property in her name, nor did she exhibit any outward signs of wealth. The blackmail idea, although it was a good thought, just didn't seem to be panning out in her case.

Johan, on the other hand, was searching for the addresses on the two people ID'd among the four being blackmailed. "You know that we'll need to contact them?"

"You mean, the cops will," Tyson said.

"Right, we're back in the USA, buddy," Galen said, chuckling, knowing it would drive Johan crazy.

"It sure cramps our style," Johan said good-naturedly.

"Well, the cops already have the information, according to Levi at least," Galen said. "So they'll be following up on the blackmail."

"That should be interesting," Johan said. "I guess we can wait for the cops and then move in for the jugular."

"You really think that the blackmailed board members had something to do with Barlow's murder?" Joy asked from across the table.

Johan had tried to sit beside her, but somehow it worked out that she was wedged between Galen and Kai. He reached over and gently nudged her foot. She smiled at him.

"I'm okay, you know?"

"You're holding up really well," he said. "We're almost done with breakfast, so let's get you to the mall and get you some clothes."

"I'm up for that," she said, as she looked at the others. "But Kai and I can do that, so you guys can go off and do your investigation."

"We could," Johan said, "but we're not too sure what we're up to yet. Finish your breakfast, and then we'll see." He watched as she looked down at her plate, still half full of scrambled eggs and potatoes. They'd ordered and been served fairly quickly, but now it looked like her appetite had waned. "You need your strength," he said gently.

She wrinkled up her nose at him. "I hear you," she said, but he just smiled.

"Don't worry about it," he replied. "Just eat what you can. You can get more later."

She nodded, took a few more bites, and then put down her fork. "I'm done," she said. "At least for now."

They nodded, and very quickly the group stood and walked out, as Johan paid the bill.

She stopped outside and turned to look up at him. "I do have money, you know? My bank account isn't empty. I don't want you paying for my meals and my hotel room."

"We'll talk about it later," he said, nudging her toward the two vehicles.

"Where are we going?" she asked, not wanting to move any closer.

"You and Kai and I are going to the mall," he said.

She frowned. "I hardly think you want to come and watch me buy lingerie," she snapped.

He gave her a heated smile and whispered, "You're wrong there," he said. "I would absolutely love to do that."

She rolled her eyes at him. "That's not what I meant."

"I just want to keep an eye on you," he said.

Considering what had been done to her apartment, she didn't argue but headed to Kai's car, where they both got in.

"So to the mall?" Kai asked.

Joy nodded. "If that's the best place, then yes."

Johan sat in the back seat and kept up a running commentary on the phone with the guys as they discussed options and information. When they pulled into the mall parking lot, he took a close look around, told the guys where they were parking and that he was heading inside with Kai and Joy.

When he got out of the vehicle, Kai looked at him and asked, "I presume you'll keep the guys in the loop?"

He nodded.

"Good. In that case then, we'll ignore you." And, with

that, Joy linked arms with Kai, and they headed inside.

Johan grinned at her spirit. If that's what she needed to do to feel better about this crappy situation, then more power to her. He trailed behind them, keeping an eye on basically everyone. It seemed ridiculous to be in such a public place, but, so far, the mall had just opened and wasn't too busy, but he knew it would grow steadier as the day wore on. He kept abreast of them as they went from store to store, picking up a few pieces here and there.

The two women were obviously best of friends, as they teased and joked and brought up memories from both sides of their friendship. He smiled and watched as they interacted and enjoyed each other.

He looked up and caught a man staring at the two women, but, when he caught Johan's gaze, the stranger immediately dropped his glance to his phone. Senses alert, Johan turned to look around to see if the guy was alone or if he had a partner with him. Sure enough, on the far side down the mall was a partner. At least Johan thought so. The young man in question walked away in the opposite direction. Johan frowned at that, and, when he turned back, the first man was gone too. He quickly noted the two and sent messages to Tyson and Galen.

Tyson responded. **Don't forget you are there with two gorgeous women.**

Johan started to laugh. Kai turned and looked at him, then frowned. "What's so funny?"

"I'm seeing boogeymen where there aren't any," he said with a smile. "I forgot that I have two beautiful women with me, and lots of men would be staring."

"As if," Joy said. But she looked happy at his comment.

The trouble was, he meant it. Now that he'd singled out

two men who had been looking at Joy, Johan could see dozens more, and he started to get even more protective.

At one point he walked over and wrapped an arm around her shoulder because a good half-dozen guys in a group stared at her. She looked at him, instantly worried. "What's the matter?"

He nudged his head to the side, and she saw the group of guys there. She smiled; they all smiled back. "They were just being friendly."

"Maybe," he said brusquely, "but I don't like it."

At that, Kai laughed and laughed. "Too funny," she said. "You're trying to protect her, but the rest of the world is liking what they see."

He growled at her. "They can like it as long as it's from a distance. I don't want anybody getting too close."

"Like you're too close?" Joy challenged him.

He glanced down at her and said, "Do you want me to leave? Do you want me to join Tyson and Galen?"

If there was a hard note in his tone, she ignored it. She reached up, patted his cheek gently. "It's really very sweet of you."

He wanted to growl again. "It's not sweet," he muttered.

"You're jealous," she said, "and I find that very interesting. But I kind of like it. As long as it doesn't get out of hand."

He rolled his eyes. "I'm not jealous."

"Of course not," she said, but she shot him a knowing look. Then she reached out and kissed him very gently on the corner of his mouth. "There. That should tell them all that I'm with you," she said.

He hated it, but he did feel better. He sighed and looped his arm with hers. "It's a very unusual feeling."

"I hear you," she said. "I can't say I've felt it very much myself."

"Yeah, well, I'm not sure I've ever felt it before," he grumbled. "And I don't like it."

"Well, you're only jealous," Kai said, "because you're insecure about the relationship." And, with that, she headed off after a beautiful dress in a window.

He stopped in the middle of the mall and tugged Joy into his arms. "You know what? She's right. I wouldn't be feeling this way if I thought you were happy to be with me."

She raised an eyebrow, her lips kicking up in the corners. "I thought we covered this ground."

"Apparently not well enough," he announced.

She kissed him gently and then kissed him again. "I'm happy to be with you," she said. "I haven't a clue what we've got going on here, but I'm happy to see where it goes."

And, with that, he had to be satisfied, but not until he got one more thing. He tugged her into his arms, so that she was locked against him, and lowered his head, kissing her thoroughly. When he finally raised his head and stared down at her completely soft and unfocused gaze, he smiled and whispered, "Now I'm happy. But satisfied? Never. Not until I have you in bed all to myself, and we can tear at the sheets like we want to."

She took a long shuddering breath, still in his arms. She seemed to get a hold of herself, stepped back, and whispered, "That time will come. But it isn't right now and certainly never in public." And, with that, she turned on her heels and headed to Kai, who stared at the two of them with a big smile on her face.

He grinned at Kai and shrugged. "Hey, I gotta lay a claim before all the other men in this place do."

"Smart of you," Kai said with a nod. "She's a sweetheart, and there have always been guys around her. But listen to me, Johan. If you ever do anything to hurt her, you will not walk away from it easily."

He just raised an eyebrow at that.

She walked up, poked him in the chest, and said, "Because I will want to know the reason why. And, if it isn't a damn good one, it's me who you'll have to deal with. God help you then."

Chapter 15

J OY LAUGHED OUT loud at the look on Johan's face after
Kai had warned him. She had been such a good friend
for a long time and had seen Joy through a multitude of
relationships and had always been protective. As Johan and
Kai walked back toward Joy, she put a smile on her face and
looked from one to the other.

"Listen," Joy said. "Don't look now, but I think that guy
has been following us."

"When did you see him first?" Johan asked, immediately
all business.

"Just before you kissed me," she said.

"That's not very long ago," Kai said.

"Maybe so," she said, "but I bet, if we duck into this
store, he'll follow us."

"He'd be foolish if he did," Johan said, "but you two go
in. I'll go on to the next one and we'll see what he does."

She slipped into the clothing store with Kai. Joy disappeared into the back, and Kai found a spot where she could
still watch the front of the store. And, sure enough, the man
walked up to the store but didn't come in. He frowned,
looked around, and then made himself at home on a bench
seat.

"So, he'll just wait for us to come out?" Joy asked.

Kai nodded. "Pretty standard procedure."

With that, and feeling bolder and a bit empowered since she'd spotted him, Joy walked out, and, deliberately ignoring him, headed toward the store that Johan had gone into. And as soon as she went inside, she watched the stranger get up and walk to that store, where he stood idly staring at the window. She looked at Johan, whose face had turned grim.

"Let's check out another store," she said. Grabbing his hand, the two of them walked out of the store right past the stranger and past several more stores before ducking inside another. She'd lost track of Kai somewhere along the way. The stranger followed at a bit of a distance. She turned to look at Johan. "So what do we do about it?"

"For the moment, we wait," he said.

"It still won't happen fast enough," she said, staring at the stranger, who even now was quite obviously waiting outside the store for them.

She dropped Johan's hand, and, before he could react, she headed outside and stepped right up to the man and asked him, "What do you want with me?"

"Who said I wanted anything to do with you?" he said in an insolent tone.

"You've been following me for the last half hour," she said. "For all I know, you're the asshole who broke into my apartment and completely destroyed everything."

"Why would anybody do that?" he asked. "Unless, of course, you were a bad girl."

A slow smile covered her face. "You don't know anything about me," she said, "and you certainly don't know what I have or have not done."

"If you're the snitch from the company, I know exactly what you are." With that, he leaned forward and whispered, "You're dead." And he turned and strode off.

"DAMN IT," JOHAN roared. "You shouldn't poke a bear like that," he snapped, but then he was gone, chasing down the mall after the stranger. He called back to Kai who yelled at him.

"I've got her."

And that was one thing he did know. Friend or not, Kai may not have been as good as he was at protecting Joy, but she was the next best thing. Besides, he didn't want to lose the one lead they'd had on this whole damn case. The fact that this guy mentioned the company and threatened Joy was huge, and that meant he was part of it. Therefore, Johan needed to get his hands on him. Plus, business aside, he wanted a chance to have "a little talk" with him.

By now the mall was jam-packed with people who were not at all cooperative about getting out of this way. He could see the stranger disappearing up ahead into a side exit. Erupting around the corner as fast as Johan could, the doors had already closed, and he saw no sign of the threatening stranger. Johan bolted outside, but, of course, a group of at least twenty people were coming and going from the mall, and still Johan saw no sign of the stranger. Johan swore up and down as he turned in a slow circle, searching for any movement that would reveal where the stranger was.

Moments later his phone buzzed. He pulled it out and grinned. "Gotcha." He hit Dial on the phone, and, when Tyson answered, he said, "You seriously got him?"

"Yep, as long as it's the same one. I'm sending a picture now."

Seconds later a photo arrived, and it was him. Johan sent a text to Tyson. **Where are you?**

Back of the parking lot on the northwest corner.

I'll go grab Kai and Joy. We'll come out and meet you.

Where are you guys parked?

Johan hated to realize that he had no damn idea, as he was completely turned around in the mall. But he was already on his way back to the women. The two of them stood in the middle of the mall aisle, talking to each other, when he finally caught sight of them. Kai looked at him, and he grinned ferociously at her.

She laughed. "Seriously, you got him?"

"Tyson did," he said, and she clapped her hands.

"Perfect." She looked over at Joy. "Come on. It's time to go."

Joy looked down at her bags, nodded, and said, "I'm probably okay for a day or two now."

He led the two of them back to the corner where he had turned, then out the exit. He called Tyson and said, "We're standing at the exit he ran from, so where are we heading?"

"Go straight ahead a good hundred yards," Tyson said. "We can see you."

With that, Johan and the two women headed in the guys' direction on foot, weaving their way through the parked vehicles as they came up to the far side. A few seconds later Johan heard a whistle. Turning, he saw where the men were standing. After a minor course correction, they joined the others minutes later.

Kai walked up and gave Tyson a big hug. "I'm so glad you were here to catch him." She peered into the car to see the guy staring at her, fury evident on his face. She just smiled at him. "Don't like it when the foot is on the other shoe, huh?"

He looked a little confused by that.

Tyson chuckled. "I think you mean, *shoe on the other foot*, hon."

"Whatever," she said, then turned back to Joy. "We have to collect our car," she said. "So I want you to stay here with the guys, and we'll meet you back—" She turned and looked at the others. "Where are we going?"

"Well, the cops want to see this guy, so maybe the police station," Tyson said.

She wrinkled up her face at that. "We can't keep him then, can we?"

"No, we can't. But maybe he'll have a little talk with us first."

The guy in the back seat swore and said, "No fucking way."

Joy looked down at him. "Why do you want me dead?"

He just glared at her.

She shrugged. "He won't talk anyway. But I've seen him at the company. I think he works in shipping."

"I wonder if he knows two people are already dead over this," Galen said.

Joy shrugged again.

"We'll meet again in a few minutes." Kai gave Joy a quick hug.

Joy looked at Galen and Johan and asked, "Where should I sit?"

"I'm driving," Galen said. "You sit in the front with me. We'll leave Johan with your new friend in the back."

She nodded. "I wouldn't be at all upset if he got beaten up a little bit on the way," she said, with half a smirk. She hopped into the front seat and twisted around to see the guy staring at her. The men had secured their prisoner's wrists, so he couldn't do too much. "He really should tell me what's going on," she said, "unless he had something to do with Barlow's death. In that case, well, he can just go to jail and rot for all I care," she said, turning around but keeping an eye on him.

There was something unnerving about having a guy like that behind her. His hands might be tied, and Johan might be beside him, but, damn, it didn't feel comfortable to her.

The guy never said a word.

Galen drove them straight to the police station. When they got out and walked inside, a detective came out, took one look, then nodded and said, "Interesting."

Two other officers came and took away the prisoner.

The detective motioned for them to enter the nearby room. He sat down and asked them a dozen questions each, and, when they were finally done, they signed their statements and left.

Chapter 16

A S SHE WALKED out of the police station, Joy asked, "Anything new on finding Barlow's murderer?"

Johan shook his head. "Not really. Still relatively early in the investigation."

She nodded. "After what our mall bully said, this guy's definitely involved."

"Well, he might be involved in whatever's going on that got Barlow killed," he said, "but that doesn't mean he killed him."

She nodded, and, back in the vehicle, she asked, "Whatever happened this morning? Did you guys go and visit those guys who were being blackmailed?"

"Well, that was the plan, but they weren't home," he said. "If you're up for it, we can go now."

"Absolutely," she said.

Galen had been there, so he knew the way. They drove up the driveway, parked, and hopped out. She noted Johan had an envelope.

"What's that?"

"We printed off copies of the photos."

"Will they think we're the blackmailers?"

"Not likely," he said, "and not for long, even if they do think that way at first."

"Right," she agreed, then shrugged.

When they got to the front door, they heard music inside. Johan stepped forward and knocked sharply on the door. The music was muted, and eventually a man came and answered the door.

He looked at them with a frown. "What's this all about?" he asked sharply.

Johan quickly identified himself, Galen, and Joy. "May we come in and speak with you for a few moments?"

Confused, the guy shook his head. "No, you can tell me whatever the hell you want right here."

"It's personal," Joy said, "but if you want us to do that here, sure."

The door opened a little wider to reveal a second man, and she recognized him from the photos as well.

She sighed. "Again, this is very personal," she said. "We can do it out here, but I think you both would feel better if we were inside."

The second man looked at the first, then opened the door wider, telling them to come in. They were led to a small formal-looking living room just inside the front door. The first man looked at them and said, "Take a seat and tell us what this is all about."

The other guy sat down and said, "I'm Mike."

She looked over at Johan and Galen, who were looking at her, so she reached for the envelope. "We didn't take these, but they did come into our possession," she said. "We would like you to know about them, in case you don't, and, if you are being blackmailed, we would very much like to know who's blackmailing you."

Both men lost all color in their faces, immediately turning pale. They stared at the envelope as if it would reach out and bite them. One of the men looked up, his gaze moving back and forth between the three of them. "Are you cops?" His voice was harsh and cutting.

Galen and Johan shook their heads. "No, we're not. We do a lot of private work though," Johan said, by way of short explanation. "This has come about in response to a man's murder and problems at a company."

"Westgroup," the man snapped.

She nodded. "I work there myself."

He turned his laser gaze on her and frowned. "I don't know you."

"I don't know most of the 240 people who work there," she said. "I doubt you do either."

He had the grace to look ashamed, and he nodded.

"In my case," she added cheerfully, "I have only been there about six weeks, so I wouldn't expect you to know me."

"What department do you work in?"

"I'm not sure I have one," she said. "I'm the inventory clerk for Westgroup and have been doing inventory, and I'm down in the basement with Phyllis and Doris, if that helps," she said. There was a moment of stillness as the men looked at each other and then back at her. She shrugged. "That obviously seemed to trigger some reaction," she said. "I just don't understand what." They looked down at the envelope again, so she asked, "Do you want to look?"

"No," Mike said. "We really don't want to look."

She sighed, dropped the envelope on the coffee table, and said, "Well, obviously you're being blackmailed then, and we would really like to know who is doing the blackmailing."

"If you've got those photos," Mike said harshly, "then you already know."

"Potentially," Johan added, "but they were hidden, so we're not so sure. And names or initials in a book don't work if we have to guess on some of it. We really don't want to guess," Johan said distinctly. "I don't know if the cops have been here yet, but they will be soon enough."

Both men settled back, and then one reached over and grabbed the other by the hand. "We've done nothing wrong."

"We're not judging you," Joy said quietly. "Personally I think blackmail is disgusting, and there is no viable reason for anybody to do this to another human being. But now a man's been murdered, and I've been threatened. At this point, I'm really tired of it all."

When she said she'd been threatened, they looked at each other again and then back at her, both frowning.

She nodded. "Yes, my place was trashed, and just this morning I was followed and threatened at the mall. He said that I'll end up dead for having spoken up about the company. In fact, the woman who had my job before me may have been killed too." At that they seemed completely surprised. She stared at them. "How involved are you in Westgroup?"

"We're not," the first man said. "We're on the board, but that's it. We're also on the board of several other big companies."

"Right," she said. "In that case, did you have anything to do with Barlow's murder?"

"Of course not," he said. "Why would we?"

"Because he was blackmailing you for one," Galen said in a sharp voice. "And that's what the police would assume when they get here too."

Both men shook their heads. "Yes, he was blackmailing

us." The one man swallowed hard. "We're not proud of caving in to blackmail, but sometimes it's what you have to do to make a problem go away. We've been together for over twenty years, but society still hasn't come to a place that would accept it."

"Well, some of it has," Joy said. "But, yes, I can see that it's still a problem, particularly in the business world."

"Exactly. I don't know how Barlow found out about us in the first place, but that's why he was still there, serving as the head of the corporation. It's where he wanted to be and what he wanted to do. We did anything we could to keep him happy."

"Including paying five thousand a month?"

"Each," Galen added.

"Yes," the first man said slowly. "We discussed it. We tried to talk him out of that money. We said only one of us could pay, but he wouldn't deal. It was both of us or none of us."

"He was also blackmailing two other men," Johan said. "I'll show you their faces, and we want to know if you know who they are." Frowning but not surprised, he held out the first photo. The men looked at it and nodded.

"They're friends of ours. But we didn't know they were being blackmailed too."

"And their names?"

"Adson Powell and Roy Drawback," he said. "They are also businessmen in prestigious positions. Unlike us though, one of them is still married to a woman."

"So, of course, if these photos were to come out, that would destroy them too." She looked at both men across from her. "And were you guys married when the photos were first taken?"

Both men nodded. "We both were. We both have children."

"Have they come around to accept your current lifestyle?"

Both men smiled. "It's been a long haul, but, yes, they have."

"Good," she said, beaming at them. "Acceptance is a wonderful gift."

"Do you know of anybody else who might have been blackmailed?" Johan asked.

"We didn't even know about these two," he said, "so, no. But, if Barlow was blackmailing us, it makes sense that maybe he was blackmailing somebody else."

"Did he ever lord it over you when you're out in public?"

"No, but then we didn't move in the same circles," Mike said stiffly. "We did a lot to go out of our way."

"Well, you're now ten thousand a month richer," Galen said. "That's a hell of a motive for murder."

"We hadn't done anything about it for the last five years," the one man said. "So why do anything now?"

And she had to admit he had a hell of a point.

JOHAN DIDN'T KNOW how to get any more information out of anybody. Nobody had, it seemed, anything more to say. "It has to be related," he muttered.

The two men nodded. "After he started this, we distanced ourselves. We always voted in favor of keeping him in place in the company, and, other than that, we were done and gone. We knew if we didn't keep him in the company, it would get worse for us."

"You never thought to call the police?" Galen asked.

They both shook their heads. "In the beginning we were both still married. We were trying to extricate ourselves nicely and figure out our own future," he said. "Police involvement would have made it a big ugly mess. The company would have suffered. We and our families would have suffered. It seemed much easier to just pay Barlow."

"Why that amount?" Joy asked. "It's not that much for guys like you, is it?"

"No, not really. Not if you're making good money, and, between the two of us, it was just an irritant."

"Maybe that's why his safe was full of cash, as if he wasn't even spending it."

"That wouldn't surprise me in the least," the first man said. "I think he did it more for revenge and because he knew he could get away with it."

"A power play," Galen said. "He could smile at you and know what he was doing, confident he had your votes and your money, and you would know what he was thinking, but you couldn't do anything about it."

She nodded. "I only met him once, but he seemed slimy."

"Good assessment," said the second man and then smiled.

She asked them, "Do you have any idea why he doesn't have any relationships himself? I wondered if he was gay too."

Both men looked at her, surprised.

She shrugged. "It doesn't really pertain to anything. I was just wondering."

"I don't know," he said. "I don't think he was gay though. He was quite homophobic."

She frowned and nodded. "It just seems strange that somebody who put so much stock in blackmailing other people's sex lives didn't have a very good one himself."

The first man looked at her with a frown and said, "Well, he had what seemed like a permanent relationship a long time ago," he said. "I don't know why that broke up."

"Yes, you do," the second man said, laughing. "She got pregnant, remember? And he wouldn't have anything to do with it."

The two men looked at each other and started talking more. "That's right. I forgot about that. Who the hell was that anyway? It was a weird name."

"Yeah, like a city or something."

She turned and looked at him. "Philly?"

Both men turned at her in surprise. "Yes. That's exactly who it was."

She stood ever-so-slowly and walked to the front door, as if her mind had completely locked on to something.

Johan called out, "Joy, what's the matter?"

"She never once mentioned a child," she said, turning. "Are you guys aware that Phyllis, who works in the basement with me, is Philly?"

Mike frowned. "Seriously? She was like a partner or something back then. There was this big foofaraw about it, and then she was gone."

"She was gone for five years, but she's back now. And has been for like nineteen years."

"Why would she do that?" the first man asked.

"I'm not sure," she said, "but maybe that's something we need to figure out. Although in truth could simply be the games she played with Barlow. Or she was part of the blackmailing. She had access to the computer system and was quite talented. Maybe she was keeping track of everyone. Nothing makes sense in their relationship."

"Do you know anything else about her pregnancy?" Johan asked them.

"No. I don't even know if she had the child," he said. "You know what rumors are like. Somebody starts them, and everybody hangs on to them. We are the byproduct of the same problem. We spent a lot of time and effort trying to keep under the radar so people don't talk about us."

She nodded. "If you think of anything else, will you give us a call?" She pulled out a piece of paper, wrote down Johan's number and her own, and placed it on the table. "It could be important."

"But it's not likely we'll come up with anything."

"No," Johan said, as he walked over to Joy, putting an arm around her shoulder, tucking her up close. "The thing is, one man's dead already, and she's been threatened, so we're doing our best to keep her alive and to solve this before something happens to her."

Understanding lit their faces. "Right."

Galen suggested something that made everybody freeze. "You also might want to consider that, now that one blackmailer is gone, you might hear from a second one."

The men stared at him in shock. "What do you mean?"

"Barlow had stacks of money for some reason," he said. "We just don't know why. Maybe he didn't care and didn't need it, but what if somebody else knew what he was doing? And what if they also had copies of the photos? For all you know, somebody else is likely to call you."

Just then one of the men's phones buzzed. He looked down at it, picked it up, and swiped his finger across the top to unlock it, then frowned at the email. "I really wish you hadn't just said that." He held up his phone. "I just got an email saying the payments will continue." He shook his head. "This shouldn't be happening," he cried out. "It should be over with."

Johan was at his side in seconds. "May I see it?" Sure enough, there was a nondescript email.

The payments will continue. Same time, same place. Just because one's dead doesn't mean the other is too.

Johan handed the phone back. "And that brings us to the next thing. How did you pay him?"

They both took a deep breath, and one spoke. "We put the money in an envelope and left it in our mailbox. When we came home, it was always gone."

"Simple, straightforward, but potentially a problem, unless somebody is out there every day waiting for it," Johan said.

"If it was on a weekend, then what?" Galen asked.

"They had to be paid on the first every month. If it was a weekday, we left it in the mailbox. If it was a weekend, we would put it there the night before. It was always gone in the morning. It's been a big thorn in our sides for years. We couldn't travel on the first or anything."

"Did you ever see who took the money? Because I sure as hell would have been standing there waiting and watching to catch him."

"We already knew who the blackmailer was," he said, "so, no, we never even looked. And honestly, in all these years, we've never seen him pick it up either."

Galen and Johan exchanged a hard look.

Joy saw it and stepped forward. "What?"

"Can you see Barlow coming here to pick up the money

every month?" Johan asked her.

She stared at him, then slowly shook her head. "No, I can't."

Johan nodded. "Neither can I. So he had a partner."

She continued, "Or he was being blackmailed too. What do both have to pay? Maybe one payment was for Barlow to keep, and the other one was for someone else to keep."

"This has to stop," the first man cried out.

Johan looked at him. "Are you ready to talk to the police now about the blackmail?"

The two men exchanged meaningful glances, then turned, standing together, their arms entwined, and nodded. "Yes," one said.

"It's time," said the other.

"Good," Johan said. "I hope we can catch the second guy before it gets any worse." He smiled at them. "The first of the month is in two days."

They both nodded. "We already have the cash too," one said grimly. "It's in the envelopes as usual."

"So you would just put it in the mailbox out front?" Johan asked.

They nodded.

He walked to the front door, flung it open, and stepped out onto the concrete. "We can set up a camera," he said. "You guys will go to work as you normally would, and we can have a video camera set up here to see who's picking up the money."

They both got excited at that idea.

He turned to Galen. "We may have to pick up some equipment though."

"Not a problem. A two-day window is huge in our world."

"It is, indeed. So today is Sunday. Tuesday's the first," he said. "We'll be back with the equipment as soon as we can, if that's okay with you."

They nodded.

"And call us if you hear anything else," Joy called out. Johan ushered her out to the vehicle. "How long will it take to get something set up?" she asked.

"Being Sunday, I'm not sure how much trouble we'll have getting something. We may have to take a drive to Levi's compound to get what we need," Johan said.

"Kai's going back anyway, isn't she? I think she has to work tomorrow," Joy said.

"So maybe Tyson can bring something back with him?"

"We'll need to hook up with them and see for sure," she said.

He nodded. "I'll give him a call."

She stood outside the car, pacing on the driveway as Johan contacted Tyson. She heard only part of the conversation, but it was short and to the point.

Minutes later he put away his phone and said, "Okay. Tyson said Kai was hoping to have dinner with you, early, like four o'clock today, and then they are heading back home tonight."

She nodded, shoving her hands in her pockets. "That works."

"Tyson will come back tomorrow morning with the gear for tracking any motion around the house."

"That sounds good." She nodded again. "So, I guess I get up and go to work in the morning?" she said, shaking her head. It all felt so damn wrong.

Chapter 17

W HEN THE NEXT morning rolled around, it felt even
worse. But she got up, dutifully got dressed, and
stood alone in her hotel room, wondering what she was
supposed to do next. When a knock came on the door, she
instinctively knew it would be Johan. She opened the door
and smiled. "You didn't have to get up just because I've got
to go to work."

"We'll work too," he reminded her gently.

She smiled. "I'd forgotten about that," she said.

"Let's go get some breakfast first," he said, "and then we
can all go together."

She nodded. "I guess there's no reason for me to have
separate wheels, is there?"

"No, I don't think so," he said.

They walked down to the hotel restaurant to find Galen
already there with a table. She quickly ordered eggs on toast,
and, when they were done, it was a quick drive to her job.

She was the first one to walk into her office. Shrugging,
she sat down at her desk and proceeded to get started on the
work that had been left from Friday.

She didn't see the men for another couple hours. All of a
sudden, she looked up to see James, her boss, standing
fretfully in her doorway.

"Good morning," she said cheerfully. He just glared at

her. She immediately fell silent and watched and waited.

"You know you can't stay here," he said.

Her heart sank. "Are you firing me?" she asked slowly.

"No, of course not," he said sarcastically. "You'll just go to the union and cause all kinds of trouble."

"Well, there are definitely laws against firing me without cause," she said, "but there's also the fact that I haven't done anything wrong."

"Haven't you?"

"No, I haven't."

He continued to glare at her for a long moment and then spun on his heels and took off. It was so bizarre.

Johan appeared moments later. "Did I just hear that right?"

"Yeah," she said, "though what it means, I don't know. He didn't come out and fire me."

"He's probably hoping you'll quit."

"Well, I would if I had a reason to," she said. "I presume for the moment that I should be here."

He looked torn, and she immediately changed her statement. "I do need to be here, at least for the moment. And they can damn well pay me a settlement if they want me to leave early, especially after the break-in and the damage at my apartment," she said. "Plus, a move will cost me a lot."

"But not too much." He then added gently, "There's not much left."

She winced. "But I still have to make that money and cough up rent for my current apartment, which is a problem."

"That's quite true," he said, and he disappeared.

Frowning at that, she finally focused on her work.

When Doris showed up, like three hours late, Joy just

smiled at her. Neither of the women said anything. Doris sat down at her desk and immediately got to work. The woman kept looking over at Phyllis's desk, but there was no sign of her.

Joy was contemplating if she should say anything to her when Doris suddenly got up and walked out of the room. Joy sank back in her chair and whispered to herself, "Everybody is so weird today."

When Doris returned, she had a coffee cup in her hand but still no smile on her face. She was a much younger woman than Phyllis, but Joy had no idea why Doris was down in this dungeon area too. Joy hoped a little conversation might ease the strained atmosphere around them. "Did you have a good weekend?" she asked in a cheerful voice.

"No," Doris snapped. "And I don't do small talk. I really don't want to talk to anybody right now." And, with that, she put in earplugs and focused on her own work.

"Wow," Joy whispered to herself. "It'll be a long day."

"They are all long days," Doris said in a snide tone. "You've got to have an end goal or life will get you."

Now she really wanted to ask what Doris's end goal was but knew the woman wouldn't say.

As the day went on, Johan and Galen received a summons to Edward's office, with the expectation that they had something to show for their time. As they walked into the penthouse floor and found the offices designated for the board members, they located Edward's office.

Edward motioned them to the two chairs across from him. "Please tell me that you have something."

"You mean, outside of the fact that the CEO was murdered?"

"Yes, dammit," he snapped. "Outside of that."

"Well, he was blackmailing several people," Johan said. "Does that help?"

Edward stared at him in shock. "What?"

"Yes," he said.

"That's just wrong."

"It is, indeed," Galen said. "So does that mean you don't know anything about it?"

"Of course I don't know anything about it," he said. "But it's crazy. No way he'd do that."

"Maybe not," Johan said. "The cops are all over it anyway. And, yes, we've tracked spare inventory coming through this place. Not necessarily drugs but items that have been moved off to the side, only to suddenly disappear, get moved over to the other warehouse. But we don't have records on the inside of receiving them. Things in the shipping area have been left quite comfortably obtuse for a long time."

"That's because our foreman is great," Edward said. "He's taking care of all that."

"Maybe, but if so, he's also looking out for himself and not for the company," Johan said. "And I think, now that things got a little bit dicey, he stepped out for a little bit."

"Are you saying he's involved?"

"No, not at all," he said. "But I don't think he checked into things as closely as he could have."

"I need to talk to him then," Edward said, jumping to his feet. "It still doesn't tell us who's involved though."

"No, it doesn't. I suspect we'll find out fairly quickly," he said. "Give us another forty-eight hours, and we should be on top of this."

Edward hemmed and hawed.

Johan said, "We've got a lot of really recent break-throughs," he said. "We just need time to tie it all together."

"Okay, I'll give you forty-eight hours," he snapped, "but that's it."

"Good enough," Johan said cheerfully; then he walked out. With Galen at his side, they walked down the hallway back to their office.

"Do you think forty-eight hours is really enough?" Galen asked.

"I suspect we'll know all about this by the time we find out who's collecting the money tomorrow," he said. "Speaking of which, have you heard from Tyson at all?"

Galen held up his phone to see a text had just come in. "He just got back to town with our stuff."

"Wow, he made good time in rush hour traffic to downtown Houston." They looked at their watches. "At lunchtime, maybe we should go set some stuff up."

"Good idea." And, with that, they had a plan.

At the doorway to their office, they stopped.

"So what about Joy?" Galen asked.

"Well, she doesn't have lunch with her, and there's no place to get it here, so why don't we take her with us?"

They walked to her office and, as they stepped in, the other woman stood there, glaring at Joy.

Joy was completely oblivious as she worked on her computer. When the guys walked in, Joy looked up, smiled, and asked, "Is it lunchtime?"

They looked over at the other woman, smiled, and Galen said, "Hello."

"Are you taking her for lunch?" the woman asked.

"Maybe," Johan said cheerfully, his gaze watchful as he studied the other woman. "Any reason not to?"

"Much better if you do," she said. "I'm not very good company right now, so I'd just as soon have the office to myself."

They looked over at the empty desk. Johan asked, "Who belongs there?"

"None of your business," the woman said coolly.

At that, he was surprised, but he nodded. "You're right. It isn't." He looked over at Joy. "Are you ready?"

She nodded, hopped up, grabbed her purse, and walked out. She called out a goodbye as she left. The other woman didn't answer. As they walked out to the car, he asked, "Is she always like that?"

Joy shook her head. "Obviously Doris must have had a shitty weekend."

Chapter 18

J OY DIDN'T KNOW if there was a bigger problem going on with Doris or not. The woman was grouchy today, but she'd never been overly friendly.

Lunch was a quick affair of sandwiches eaten on the run. They headed to the house of the two blackmailed men from the board. There they met up with Tyson, who had brought the equipment from the compound. They had a sandwich for him too. They quickly set up cameras on the outside and then another pointing to the driveway as well.

"Too bad we don't have one in my office," she muttered. "I'm forever feeling that somebody is staring at me."

"Still?"

She nodded. "Yeah, it's kind of creepy."

"Well, I have spare equipment now, if you want to set something up."

"We'd have to do it without anybody else knowing," she said.

When they got back to her office, thankfully it was empty. "Perfect. No time like the present," Tyson said.

After a quick look around, he found a place just above the door where he could fit the discrete camera against a bit of the molding that went around the doorframe. Within seconds he had it up and installed. He said, "I'll keep the feed on my phone for now, just for testing."

She nodded. "Fine with me."

And, with that, he said, "I'll disappear so I don't attract more attention."

She laughed, watching him leave, now looking at Johan and Galen. "Coffee's around the corner, if you two want some."

"You know what? We never did find the coffee," Galen said. "You want to show us?"

She nodded, then led the way to the little lunchroom. As usual, there was a pot, but it was empty. She thought the others prided themselves on creating that problem. She quickly put on a fresh pot, and, while they stood here, waiting for it to drip, Johan's phone rang.

He answered it. "Hey, Tyson. What's up?" He listened a moment. "Oh, really? That's interesting," he said. He shot Galen a hard look and quietly said, "Keep her here." And, with that, he disappeared.

She turned, coffee cups in hand. Staring at Galen, she asked, "What was that all about?"

He shrugged, but his face was hard. He took the cups from her, poured coffee in them, and said, "I'm not sure we'll get much chance to drink this."

She frowned, looked at the coffee, looked at him, and said, "Is it my office?"

"I don't know, but Tyson just called, and Johan took off."

"I want to go see," she said abruptly.

"And I'd agree with that," he said, "but I'll carry the coffee."

She let him carry the three cups back to her office. Johan stopped her outside the door. She looked at him with a frown and asked, "Why can't I go in?"

He sighed. "You can go in," he said, "but you won't like what you see."

She stepped into the office, not sure what to expect. She found Tyson pulling down a camera that had been set into the ceiling tiles. She stared at him in shock. "So somebody *was* watching?"

He nodded grimly. "We've just got clearance from Edward to track it back," he said. "It goes to Barlow's office."

"Wow," she said, "that's just bizarre."

"Maybe not," he said. "We're thinking it was probably directed at Phyllis more so than you."

She looked at where Phyllis sat and then her own desk and nodded. "That says a lot about their relationship. Whether he was keeping an eye on her or it was something they liked between them."

"Twisted in oh-so-many ways," he said. "We also asked Edward to contact Phyllis to see why she didn't show up today."

Joy looked at him and wrinkled up her face. "Please don't tell me something happened to her."

"We're not at all sure," he said. "He didn't get an answer, so somebody has gone to take a look."

She turned around in a wide motion. "We could go check."

"No, the cops have been called in. They'll do a welfare check to see if she's okay."

She reached up to massage her forehead when Doris walked in. "People appear to be concerned about Phyllis," she said to Doris. "Have you heard anything from her?"

Doris looked surprised, then shrugged. "How the hell would I know?" she said. She looked at the electronic equipment and said, "What the hell is going on here?"

"Just something from the board," Tyson said and walked out with it.

Doris didn't sit back down again. "More weird games between those two."

"Which two?" Johan asked.

"Phyllis and her lover."

"Are they still lovers?"

"Yes. That is a very weird game they play. Been together since forever."

Joy turned to look at Johan. He shrugged. "Hey, I don't get involved with other people's sex lives," he muttered.

"Well, theirs is bizarre anyway," Doris snapped.

"How bizarre?"

"No clue," Doris said and clammed up. "I have work to do, so, if you're not working here, get out of my office."

At that, Joy sent Johan back out again. She sat back down at her desk and got to work. She was hoping there would be an opportunity to talk to Doris about Phyllis. "You seem like you are pretty good friends with Phyllis."

"Hell no," she said. "Can't stand the woman." But her tone was absentminded, as if she was busy with her office stuff and hadn't really considered what the question was all about.

With that, Joy didn't really know what else to say.

When Johan popped his head in about a half an hour later, the look on his face caused her to suck back her breath.

"So," he said. "Phyllis has been found, and she's dead."

Doris looked up and blanched. "Seriously?"

"Yes."

Doris just sat there in shock, but that was pretty well how Joy felt too. Joy asked no one in particular, "I wonder if it was the same person who killed Barlow."

"Of course it was," Doris said. "Like I said, those two were involved and have been for a really long time."

"Anything illegal in their involvement?"

"Well, it started off as just Phyllis I think, but then Barlow got involved."

"What was she doing?"

"Stealing shit. But then so was Barlow. That's how his company was built. He built it as a shell company to run a bunch of other shit around and through this place."

The words just spilled from her mouth, and Johan stared at her in shock. "And you know that how?"

Doris shrugged and didn't say anything.

"If you know something," Joy said, "please speak up."

"Why the hell should I?" she said. "Speaking up doesn't do any good." With that, she grabbed her purse and sweater, then said, "I'm taking the rest of this day as a sick day. Obviously I'm overcome with grief," she said sarcastically; then she turned and walked out.

Johan stared at Joy.

"I've never heard her speak like that before," Joy said. "And how would she know any of this?"

"She wouldn't," Johan said. "Unless she's involved in something."

"Well, that doesn't mean she's involved in the thefts."

"Maybe she was involved in something else though."

"The blackmail?" she asked. "Does that mean Phyllis was doing the blackmailing too?"

"I don't know," he said. "I guess it depends on who shows up for the money tomorrow. If anybody does."

"Right. So who else then?"

JOHAN DIDN'T LIKE what was happening. Things were coming to a head, and it wasn't in a good way. He headed back to his desk and started researching Doris. A bit of an enigma was involved in that woman. He went through the staff records, pulling open her personnel file. She'd asked for some shrink time at one point, and, other than that, she seemed to be a model worker. She'd worked for the company for five years. So why the hell was she still working in the basement?

He knew other people would say that it wasn't a punishment to be down here, but, as far as he was concerned, it was. There were a lot nicer places to work in this huge building. Unless she wanted to be close to where the smuggling was happening? The fact that she'd accused Phyllis of theft and Barlow of smuggling almost made sense. Even if it was a shell company, Barlow would need somebody, like Phyllis, to give him a hand moving stuff. She was also his accounting spy.

Johan looked up to see Galen walking in.

"Any news?" Galen asked, sitting down at his desk.

"Yes," Johan said, "but the cops will be here anytime now. According to Doris, Phyllis and Barlow were into theft and smuggling, using the company as a shell."

"In that case, it sure would be nice to get into her laptop before the cops get here."

"That's what I was thinking."

Galen opened his laptop and said, "Give me a minute." Very quickly he managed to access her laptop remotely.

Johan stood behind Galen as they went through her folders, and everything appeared to be pretty standard. "So there's nothing jumping out at me. How about you?"

"*Hmm.* Look at this." Galen pointed out a folder on one

of the servers that had a naming pattern inconsistent with the rest. He clicked on it, and it took him to several more folders, and, by the time he finished clicking through, he found pictures of a little girl. Pictures of a girl growing up but always just pictures of the girl, never with a parent. "Do you think that's Phyllis's daughter?"

"It's possible."

Another folder had pictures of the child at school. The photos had clearly been separated into groups and kept in different folders. One for home, one for school, and one for visits. They found a few pictures of Phyllis with the little girl.

"Visits," Johan said. "Probably registered visits, so maybe the child was raised by an adoptive family or a foster home."

They got to the end of the pictures, when Johan reached out. "Hold it. Look right there." They looked at the last photo. "Does she remind you of anyone?"

Galen sat back and whistled. "Yeah, the woman who just left."

They bolted back to Joy's office to see Joy still sitting there, working away. Johan sighed with relief. "So, we have another connection," he said. "It looks like Doris might very well be Phyllis's daughter."

Joy stared at him in shock, her gaze going from one empty desk to the other. "Seriously?"

He nodded. "But we don't know for sure. We only have photos of her when she was quite a bit younger."

"I don't think she's all that old," she said slowly. "I think she dresses dowdy to *un*impress, if you know what I mean."

"What? She does that?" Johan asked. "On purpose?"

"Maybe she was blackmailing Barlow." Joy looked from Johan to Galen.

Johan shook his head. "Doris blackmailing Barlow? Or

Phyllis blackmailing Barlow? Either way, doesn't fly for me. Barlow's heartless. He wouldn't care if the world knew he had a daughter who he disowned before birth. But it would be karmic justice if he were being blackmailed by someone. If so, then he's blackmailing others so he can get the money to pay his own blackmailer?"

"It's possible." Galen shrugged. "It would explain the cash in his safe."

Johan paused. "What seems *more* probable is that Barlow was stockpiling money and jewels to make a run for it, now that the heat's turning up on their smuggling op."

"Yeah, now I can see that," Galen stated. "I wonder if he would've taken Phyllis with him."

"*Huh.* Doubtful. I don't see him as the loyal type," Johan stated.

"That adoption would have been tough," Galen noted.

"Yeah," Joy said. "On both women. Somehow I think Phyllis cared about Doris, in her own limited way, yet not so much that Doris cared for her mom, who abandoned her early in her life."

"Seems Phyllis's death may have made Doris care a bit," Galen commented.

"Too little, too late," Johan noted. Just then Johan's phone rang. "This is one of the guys where we set up the cameras at his mailbox."

"What's up with him?"

"Hello? This is Johan."

"We got emails. He wants the money today!"

"Okay. So go ahead and put the money in the box," Johan said. "We've already got it set up."

"Oh, good," he said in relief. "We didn't know if it was good to go or what."

"Are you at work?"

"Yes," he said.

"Then come home as usual and put the money in the box. We'll keep track of it and be in touch. Try to keep your cool and don't do anything suspicious."

"Done," he said and hung up.

Johan looked at Joy. "I wonder if it's a coincidence that Doris left here early."

Joy sat back and stared. "That would be a little too unbelievable."

"Not really," he said. "We've often wondered if there was more than just one team at work here."

"Well, I think the smuggling was one team, but I'm not sure what is going on now with the blackmailing part."

"Exactly." He held out his hand. "Sounds like you're done for the day."

"I have a lot of work to do," she said, "and if these two aren't here, I can—"

Just then Edward burst in. "What the hell is going on?" He looked completely frazzled.

"Phyllis has been murdered," Johan said, "in case you hadn't heard the news. Likely by the same person who murdered Barlow. Considering the camera down here facing Phyllis, which fed back to Barlow, that would make sense."

Edward just shook his head. "I don't understand," he said. "I really don't understand."

"Well, according to Doris," Joy said, motioning to the seat beside her, "the two of them—Barlow and Phyllis—have been smuggling from the company for many years. Westgroup was originally set up as a shell company to move materials that he could then sell on the black market. He had to legitimize it in order to make it survive. Then he moved the smuggling operation into a much smaller scenario. All of that with help from Phyllis."

Edward's skin faded even more and took on a waxy pallor. "This will ruin us," he said. "You know that? This will ruin us."

"Well, this isn't the first time it's come up though, has it?" Johan asked, crossing his arms. "The woman who was here before Joy brought up findings indicative of theft."

Edward frowned and shrugged. "But she wasn't here very long."

"No," Joy said. "She was also killed in a hit-and-run before she could do any more."

He gasped, his hand going to his heart. With that, he turned and bolted.

"You know this just might lead to him resigning from the board today too," she said in a conversational tone. "I feel sorry for the rest of the people who work here, but it sounds like a lot of people will jump ship really fast."

"Rats always jump ship as soon as there's any sign of trouble," Johan said. "Don't worry about it. They also have a really good survival instinct."

She looked around, sighed, and said, "I have to leave, don't I?"

"The sooner, the better," he said. "So get up and log off. Let's see if we can sort all this out today."

Chapter 19

O UTSIDE IN THE front seat of the vehicle, she asked, "Where are we going?"

"We're just waiting to find out who comes tonight," he said and nodded toward Galen in the back seat behind him. "The blackmailer emailed the board members to move up the money drop by a day."

"What are you saying?" She twisted around to see Galen, watching a laptop. "Ah," she said. "Are you monitoring who's picking up the money?"

"Yep. And so are the cops." Just then Galen whispered, "And here's a vehicle." He held up the laptop a little bit so they could see what the camera saw. "It's a woman, sure enough. Is that Doris?"

"Yeah, it looks like her," Johan said.

"Watch this." Galen chuckled.

Doris walked up, reached her hand in the mailbox, and pulled out two envelopes. She seemed completely unconcerned, as if she expected them to be there, having done this many times. She walked back to her car, and, before she had a chance to do anything more, she was surrounded by cops.

"Got her," Galen said, with a note of satisfaction. He smiled and closed the laptop. "Okay, now what do you want to do?"

She just stared at him. "So, that's the blackmail issue,

but what about the thefts?"

"I highly suspect it's all involved," Johan said. "And with Phyllis and Barlow both dead, that should take care of smuggling element."

"So it's over then? But I don't feel like it's over," she said.

"I'm not sure that it's all over," he said.

Just then there was a knock on the window. Johan turned to see Edward there. Johan opened the door, hopped out, and Joy looked on as Edward pulled a small handgun and put it against Johan's jaw.

She cried out, "Oh, my God! Edward, what are you doing?"

"Johan's ruined everything," Edward said. "And so have you." Edward shoved Johan back into the driver's seat and opened the back door, quickly pointing the gun at Galen, getting him to move over so Edward could get into the back. "Now get us out of here," he said to Johan, holding the gun against Galen.

"Nice .22 you got there, Edward. So what's your plan here?" Johan asked as he started up the vehicle.

"I don't know," Edward said, "but I've got somebody picking up some money for me, and it will help me get away."

"So, Doris is working for you?" Johan asked.

"Of course not," he said. "She's my lover." He sneered.

"Jesus," Joy said.

"She disguises that pretty well, doesn't she?" Edward said, laughing. "We didn't want anybody at the company to know."

"Of course," Johan said. "So you know that Phyllis was her mother, right?"

Edward stopped and stared. "How did you guys figure that out?"

"You'd be surprised," Johan replied. "So that's how Doris knew about the blackmail?"

"Of course. It's all in the family."

"And how many more people are you blackmailing?"

"Lots," he said, "but that's not your problem or your business."

"And the theft in the company?"

"Well, it's been going on for twenty years," he said, "but you're pretty well bringing that to a grinding halt. Once the cops get involved in it, we'll be forced to change our plans. We'll up the blackmail to help compensate. Besides, moving the drugs was getting harder and harder anyway. So that operation was much diminished compared to what we used to have."

"And what about Chelsea, the woman who worked my desk before me?"

He shrugged. "Well, she had to be taken out, did she not? That was easy. Of course Philly took care of her. Even Doris took my truck and tried to run you down. Only she missed."

"And what about Ricardo? What's his involvement?"

"So you know about him too? He's my IT guy. Had to have a hacker in my pocket. Just paid him to do some super secret stuff for the company. The kid loved it. Thought he would go far. I'll have to deal with him too, damn." He shrugged. "Or not. Once I'm gone, he'll be the fool who's been hacking the company database. He'll take the fall for that. Same as the idiot at the mall. Why would I pay him to do more when he had failed already? He trashed your apartment but was supposed to take you out too, and he didn't. I had to put the damn bugs in myself. Just like I had to kill Barlow and Phyllis. Still, in for a penny, in for a pound. Of course Ricardo drove a friend's truck to try and run her off the road." And he gave Joy a smile that made her shiver.

"And now? What do you plan to do with me?"

"Same deal as the others but with its own twist," he said cheerfully. "You know what? We'll drive to a nice lonely spot. Three bullets and you'll all be gone. I'll leave the gun behind. Doris will pick me up, and we'll leave. I already resigned from the company, so we're good to go. It's not like her job was of any value anyway. Phyllis and Barlow are also gone, and, by the time the media gets ahold of all this, it'll blow up beautifully." He laughed and laughed. "So, keep driving," he said, "or I'll blow Galen's head apart."

She watched as Johan drove carefully, following Edward's instructions. "We don't have much gas, you know?" she said.

Edward leaned toward the front seat and frowned when he checked the gas gauge. "So pull into a gas station. We'll have to get some at least. We have a bit of a drive ahead."

Johan obediently pulled into the next gas station.

Edward immediately sat up. "Now watch it," he said. "Anything funny and he'll get the first bullet, and she'll get the second."

He nodded slowly, got out, opened the gas tank, and started filling it up.

She wasn't sure what he was doing, but it seemed like something else was going on. His hands were a little too busy. He had his phone out, texting. With that, she settled back and smiled, knowing Johan would appreciate it if she were to distract the gunman in the back seat. "So tell me,

Edward," she said. "All this trouble, why?"

"What do you mean, why? For money," he said. "Originally we were all planning on getting rid of the company and going off to retire early. Of course Barlow and Phyllis had their weird little relationship thing going on still, but—"

"What split them up way back when?"

"Her getting pregnant of course. He couldn't handle that at all."

"Of course not," she said, with a sigh. "That would be way too much to ask of him."

He shrugged and said, "Whatever. It was all fine until you came on board. If you hadn't been so damn nosy, it wouldn't have been a problem."

"Maybe."

And just like that, the door opened beside Edward. Galen grabbed Edward's gun, while Johan hit Edward hard in the temple. He made a weird strangled sound, but he never fired a shot, as he slowly sagged into the seat.

Within minutes, the cops pulled up and circled them. Joy got out of the front seat, ran around, and threw herself into Johan's arms.

"Oh, my God," she whispered.

He held her close, kissing her neck, her cheek, and her forehead.

"Oh, my God. Oh, my God." She reached up and grabbed his head, then pulled him down and kissed him hard.

When he lifted his head, he smiled. "Now that's what I'm talking about."

She laughed and then started to cry, and he just held her close.

MUCH LATER THAT evening they finally said goodbye to Tyson again and walked back to the hotel. They'd gone to dinner around the corner from where they were staying. When she got to her room, she waited for Johan to join her. He stopped at the doorway and frowned. She smiled at him. "Of course you're coming in, aren't you?"

He stepped in and closed the door. "I don't want to push you."

"No, we're well past that now." She threw herself into his arms and just held him close. "Do you know how close we came to dying today?" she cried out.

He nodded and pulled her back into his arms. "I'm sorry. I would have done anything to spare you from experiencing that."

"You did everything you could, and the bottom line is, we're all safe, and that's what matters." She reached up and kissed him deeply.

He tried to slow her down, but she wasn't having it. Her hands were busy on his shirt buttons, and, before he realized it, she was taking it off his shoulders.

"Whoa, whoa, whoa," he said. "We have time."

"Good," she said, "because I intend to make very good use of that time."

His eyebrows shot up, and she just grinned as she stepped back, crossed her arms, and lifted her shirt over her head, tossing it. She shucked her pants just as fast, and, just like that, she stood there in sandals, tiny little white cotton briefs, and a bra.

He reached out, stroking along the top of the elastic and said, "I don't remember you buying those."

"Good," she said. "Then it's a surprise."

He swallowed hard and nodded, his hands going to his

belt. But she took his hands away and quickly undid the belt for him. When she went to slide the zipper down on his jeans, her hand slid over the bulge, gently caressing and stroking, stopping for a moment to squeeze.

He shuddered. "I think this will be a hell of a night," he muttered.

"I know it'll be a hell of a night." She took off her bra, kicked off her sandals and the scrap of cotton briefs with it, and raced to the bed. Pulling back the sheets, she kneeled in the center of the bed and opened her arms.

He didn't know what the hell happened, but she was like a whirlwind. He walked toward her—proud, erect, and dying for the experience he'd been looking forward to since he'd first met her.

She threw herself into his arms and whispered, "Love me, Johan. Make me feel alive. Remind me why we went through all this shit these last few days."

"How about I do even better than that?" he said. "How about I love you and remind you that life is so much more than what we went through this week." And, with that, he gently kissed her, but the fire and passion between them soared and seared as they came together from hips to chest in a fury of skin and nerves. Myriad sensations shuddered and rolled through them both.

She sighed, then whispered, "I need you so badly."

"Lie down," he whispered.

She immediately dropped down on top of the sheet and opened her arms.

He slowly covered her, but, when she started to pull him to her, she spread her thighs wide, hoping he would come to her immediately. He shook his head.

"Not just yet."

She groaned but lay shuddering under his ministrations as he stoked the fires within her. He didn't want it over quite so fast. Not their first time, not like that. So he kissed and caressed her, his fingers stroking until he slid one finger inside her, and her hips shoved upward, sending it deeper as she cried out.

She melted all around him, and he watched with joy as her passion overtook her, and she let go, completely unfazed and natural in her response. When she lay shuddering before him, she opened her eyes.

"Now I want to be with you."

He gently fitted himself against her entrance and carefully slid deep inside. She cried out, her body coming apart yet again. Still shuddering, she reached up and whispered, "Dear God, I don't know what you've done to me," she said, "but this is too damn perfect."

He slid right to the hilt and slowly moved again, driving them both faster and faster to the peak. When she came apart in his arms for a third time, he finally allowed himself to relax and to let his own release find him.

When he collapsed beside her, his head hitting the pillow, he whispered, "I think you killed me."

"No," she said. "I didn't. But I might by morning."

Laughing, he opened his arms and held her close. "Bring it on," he whispered. "Bring it on."

Epilogue

W HEN GALEN ALRICK walked into the kitchen of Ice and Levi's compound, he was feeling pretty decent. As Harrison looked up at him with a grumble on his face, Galen's eyebrows shot up. "Well, I thought it was a good day," he said laughingly.

"While you guys solved your problem," Harrison said, "we got the brakes put on ours."

"Yeah, you were supposed to give us a hand, weren't you? Good thing we didn't need it." Just enough gentle rivalry existed between the two groups for him to want to rib Harrison a little bit over this one. Galen originally had worked for Bullard for a good seven years, but now he was doing an exchange program here, and he wasn't exactly sure what his future held. He'd already talked to Bullard about it prior to leaving, wondering if it wasn't time to move on and to do something else. Bullard had just shrugged, smiled, and told him to come back when he wanted more work, saying he would always be welcome.

But then they'd heard about Johan's decision to come and work for Ice, and Galen had jumped on board with that, wondering if the change would be enough for him. Now he was here, and that was a darn fast job he had just completed with Johan, not at all what Galen was used to, but it was kind of fun.

"Did Johan come back with you?" Harrison asked.

Galen snorted. "Well, he stayed to help Joy take care of the last things she needed to do."

"Did she quit?"

"She got a nice little paycheck as thanks," he said. "Kai went over for a couple extra days to lend a hand, but everything in Joy's apartment got trashed, so there really wasn't anything to pack up. But it had to be hauled off, and Joy had some banking and whatnot she wanted to do, plus several meetings with the company."

"Did she want to leave? At least she had a job there."

"Exactly. She had a job. It wasn't a great job or what she wanted to do, but it was something that paid the rent for the time being. That's part of the reason why we all were there. We had to talk with the apartment manager and the guy she had subleased the apartment from. Not to mention the cops. So they dropped me off yesterday, and they are looking for a place for her now, something within a ten-mile radius of the compound, if possible."

"You know she could probably move in here in the meantime."

"I don't think she's too comfortable with that, at least not yet," Galen said. He walked over, poured himself a cup of coffee, and set it down beside Harrison. Then he walked back over to the coffee area. "Living here is also the best part. These are some serious side benefits." He looked at the pan of fresh warm cinnamon buns, the icing still melted all over the top.

"That's the second tray already," Harrison said good-naturedly. "I don't know how the two of them do it, but they just keep the food coming."

"And it's a divine system," he said. He gently eased a

cinnamon bun off the big tray and put it on his plate and came back over. He sat down and said, "Working here isn't exactly what I thought it would be like. I may need extra workout time to keep all this food in check."

"That's because you had a simple job assignment this last time," Harrison said with a snort. "Some of the jobs are very, very ugly."

"I do ugly," Galen said comfortably.

"I'm glad to hear that," came a sharp voice from the other side of the room. He looked up to see Ice walking toward him with a clipboard.

He grinned. "Do you ever run out of work for us?"

"Not if I can help it," she said. She sat down somewhat awkwardly, already protecting her unborn babe, while her belly remained unchanged. The fact that she was pregnant in the middle of all this chaos was amazing, and it also showed just how messed up the world was that she was as busy as this while she was pregnant.

"Isn't it time for you to get an assistant?"

"I have at least two or three of them now," she complained good-naturedly. "This will ground me for a few months, but it shouldn't be too bad after that."

"I'm sure the payoff is worth it," Galen said.

She beamed at him. "It certainly is in my case," she said as she tapped her clipboard. "So, you can do ugly, can you?"

"Yes. I can also go and help Harrison on this art job."

"Nope. We've been told to butt out of that one. The insurance company is bringing in somebody, and the cops don't want everybody crossing lines, so it's on hold again."

"The fresher it is—"

She shrugged. "I can't do anything about it. So, in the meantime, Harrison'll work on it on his own, just quietly in the background. Meanwhile, Galen, you are heading off to Germany to join Zack."

Harrison sucked in his breath and glared at Ice.

She just smiled benignly back at him.

"Did you arrange this with Zoe?" Harrison asked. "To keep me in town?"

"Nope," she said. "But you wanted the art job, so you got the art job."

"You said it was on hold though," he protested.

"But you also know it'll come back on our plate, so there's no point in you being completely green when that happens. You might as well get up to speed now."

"It could be a waste of time and money," he warned.

She smiled. "It could be, but we've rarely had any of those, so that's your job."

He nodded. "In that case, I'll get to it. I suspect a lot of it's cyberstuff anyway." He poured himself another cup of coffee and disappeared.

Galen looked at her and smiled. "You get jobs of all kinds here, don't you?"

"I do," she said.

"And who's Zack?"

"Somebody we've been looking at working with us for a couple years," she said. "He's in Germany right now, waiting for you."

"Then I better get packing," he said, as he ripped off another piece of the cinnamon bun and sat here quite comfortably, in absolutely no rush.

"You fly out in two and a half hours," she said, "so you'll be tight for time anyway."

He nodded. "I'm already packed, so I will sit here and enjoy this."

She nodded. "Take one with you, if you want."

"I might do that," he said and motioned at her clipboard. "You going to give me any idea what I'm going into?"

She looked up at him, and her eyes started to twinkle.

His stomach fell. "Please don't let it be some sort of ridiculous waste of time," he said.

"So, how do you feel about beer?"

He brightened. "I love beer. And isn't that a huge cliché? Just send me to Germany to look after some beer issues?"

"Well, a lot of free beer goes with the job," she said, laughing.

"Now that I'm up for," he said, "but you're still not talking."

"One of the biggest breweries is having some issues. I don't have all the details, but Zack asked for backup. So you're it."

"If you say so," he said. He popped the last piece of the cinnamon bun into his mouth and picked up the cup and threw back the last of his coffee. "Am I driving in and leaving the vehicle at the airport?"

She shook her head. "Nope. Levi's taking you in. He's got to pick up a bunch of shit too."

"Look at you guys," he said. "The owners of the company, and the big bwana's at the top of the pile, and you're both grounded."

She shrugged. "We are grounded but, this time, by choice." She patted her tummy.

This concludes Book 21 of Heroes for Hire: Johan's Joy.

Read about Galen's Gemma: Heroes for Hire, Book 22

Heroes for Hire: Galen's Gemma (Book #22)

Galen had plans to kick back and relax, but Levi needs someone to help out Zack, a friend of his. When Levi asks Galen, he's game. There's a little too much sugary sweet true love going on at the compound for him and his single state to handle. Then he meets Gemma and her sister, the real reason Zack was looking for help.

Gemma learned a long time ago how to handle her sister and her niece. When the two end up in deep trouble, Gemma drops everything and takes charge. But it's dangerous, and she needs help. Galen wasn't what she had in mind, but her heart is open and willing. Her body? Well, it's

good to go when a meet-and-greet leads to love at first sight.

Only the situation is dangerous, and she has to stay focused—until the truth comes out, and she finds out what's really at stake.

Find Book 22 here!

To find out more visit Dale Mayer's website.

http://smarturl.it/DMSGalen

Other Military Series by Dale Mayer

SEALs of Honor

Heroes for Hire

SEALs of Steel

The K9 Files

The Mavericks

Bullards Battle

Hathaway House

Terkel's Team

Ryland's Reach: Bullard's Battle (Book #1)

Welcome to a new stand-alone but interconnected series from Dale Mayer. This is Bullard's story—and that of his team's. All raw, rough, incredibly capable men who have one goal: to find out who was behind the attack on their leader, before the attacker, or attackers, return to finish the job.

Stay tuned for more nonstop action as the men narrow down their suspects ... and find a way to let love back into their own empty lives.

His rescue from the ocean after a horrible plane explosion was his top priority, in any way, shape, or form. A small sailboat and a nurse to do the job was more than Ryland hoped for.

When Tabi somehow drags him and his buddy Garret onboard and surprisingly gets them to a naval ship close by, Ryland figures he'd used up all his luck and his friend's too. Sure enough, those who attacked the plane they were in weren't content to let him slowly die in the ocean. No. Surviving had made him a target all over again.

Tabi isn't expecting her sailing holiday to include the rescue of two badly injured men and then to end with the loss of her beloved sailboat. Her instincts save them, but now she finds it tough to let them go—even as more of Bullard's team members come to them—until it becomes apparent that not only are Bullard and his men still targets ... but she is too.

B ULLARD CHECKED THAT the helicopter was loaded with their bags and that his men were ready to leave.

He walked back one more time, his gaze on Ice. She'd never looked happier, never looked more perfect. His heart ached, but he knew she remained a caring friend and always would be. He opened his arms; she ran into them, and he held her close, whispering, "The offer still stands."

She leaned back and smiled up at him. "Maybe if and when Levi's been gone for a long enough time for me to forget," she said in all seriousness.

"That's not happening. You two, now three, will live long and happy lives together," he said, smiling down at the woman knew to be the most beautiful, inside and out. She would never be his, but he always kept a little corner of his heart open and available, in case she wanted to surprise him and to slide inside.

And then he realized she'd already been a part of his heart all this time. That was a good ten to fifteen years by now. But she kept herself in the friend category, and he understood because she and Levi, partners and now parents, were perfect together.

Bullard reached out and shook Levi's hand. "It was a hell of a blast," he said. "When you guys do a big splash, you really do a *big* splash."

Ice laughed. "A few days at home sounds perfect for me now."

"It looks great," he said, his hands on his hips as he surveyed the people in the massive pool surrounded by the palm trees, all designed and decked out by Ice. Right beside all the war machines that he heartily approved of. He grinned at her. "When are you coming over to visit?" His gaze went to Levi, raising his eyebrows back at her. "You guys should come over for a week or two or three."

"It's not a bad idea," Levi said. "We could use a long holiday, just not yet."

"That sounds familiar." Bullard grinned. "Anyway, I'm off. We'll hit the airport and then pick up the plane and head home." He added, "As always, call if you need me."

Everybody raised a hand as he returned to the helicopter and his buddy who was flying him to the airport. Ice had volunteered to shuttle him there, but he hadn't wanted to take her away from her family or to prolong the goodbye. He hopped inside, waving at everybody as the helicopter lifted. Two of his men, Ryland and Garret, were in the back seats. They always traveled with him.

Bullard would pick up the rest of his men in Australia. He stared down at the compound as he flew overhead. He preferred his compound at home, but damn they'd done a nice job here.

With everybody on the ground screaming goodbye, Bullard sailed over Houston, heading toward the airport. His two men never said a word. They all knew how he felt about Ice. But not one of them would cross that line and say anything. At least not if they expected to still have jobs.

It was one thing to fall in love with another man's woman, but another thing to fall in love with a woman who was so unique, so different, and so absolutely perfect that you knew, just knew, there was no hope of finding anybody else like her. But she and Levi had been together way before Bullard had ever met her, which made it that much more heartbreaking.

Still, he'd turned and looked forward. He had a full roster of jobs himself to focus on when he got home. Part of him was tired of the life; another part of him couldn't wait to head out on the next adventure. He managed to run everything from his command centers in one or two of his locations. He'd spent a lot of time and effort at the second one and kept a full team at both locations, yet preferred to spend most of his time at the old one. It felt more like home to him, and he'd like to be there now, but still had many more days before that could happen.

The helicopter lowered to the tarmac, he stepped out, said his goodbyes and walked across to where his private plane waited. It was one of the things that he loved, being a pilot of both helicopters and airplanes, and owning both birds himself.

That again was another way he and Ice were part of the same team, of the same mind-set. He'd been looking for another woman like Ice for himself, but no such luck. Sure, lots were around for short-term relationships, but most of them couldn't handle his lifestyle or the violence of the world that he lived in. He understood that.

The ones who did had a hard edge to them that he found difficult to live with. Bullard appreciated everybody's being alert and aware, but if there wasn't some softness in the women, they seemed to turn cold all the way through.

As he boarded his small plane, Ryland and Garret following behind, Bullard called out in his loud voice, "Let's go, slow pokes. We've got a long flight ahead of us."

The men grinned, confident Bullard was teasing, as was his usual routine during their off-hours.

"Well, we're ready, not sure about you though …" Ryland said, smirking.

"We're waiting on you this time," Garret added with a chuckle. "Good thing you're the boss."

Bullard grinned at his two right-hand men. "Isn't that the truth?" He dropped his bags at one of the guys' feet and said, "Stow all this stuff, will you? I want to get our flight path cleared and get the hell out of here."

They'd all enjoyed the break. He tried to get over once a year to visit Ice and Levi and same in reverse. But it was time to get back to business. He started up the engines, got confirmation from the tower. They were heading to Australia for this next job. He really wanted to go straight back to Africa, but it would be a while yet. They'd refuel in Honolulu.

Ryland came in and sat down in the copilot's spot, buckled in, then asked, "You ready?"

Bullard laughed. "When have you ever known me *not* to be ready?" At that, he taxied down the runway. Before long he was up in the air, at cruising level, and heading to Hawaii. "Gotta love these views from up here," Bullard said. "This place is magical."

"It is once you get up above all the smog," he said. "Why Australia again?"

"Remember how we were supposed to check out that newest compound in Australia that I've had my eye on? Besides the alpha team is coming off that ugly job in Sydney. We'll give them a day or two of R&R then head home."

"Right. We could have some equally ugly payback on that job."

Bullard shrugged. "That goes for most of our jobs. It's the life."

"And don't you have enough compounds to look after?"

"Yes I do, but that kid in me still looks to take over the world. Just remember that."

"Better you go home to Africa and look after your first two compounds," Ryland said.

"Maybe," Bullard admitted. "But it seems hard to not continue expanding."

"You need a partner," Ryland said abruptly. "That might ease the savage beast inside. Keep you home more."

"Well, the only one I like," he said, "is married to my best friend."

"I'm sorry about that," Ryland said quietly. "What a shit deal."

"No," Bullard said. "I came on the scene last. They were always meant to be together. Especially now they are a family."

"If you say so," Ryland said.

Bullard nodded. "Damn right, I say so."

And that set the tone for the next many hours. They landed in Hawaii, and while they fueled up everybody got off to stretch their legs by walking around outside a bit as this was a small private airstrip, not exactly full of hangars and tourists. Then they hopped back on board again for takeoff.

"I can fly," Ryland offered as they took off.

"We'll switch in a bit," Bullard said. "Surprisingly, I'm doing okay yet, but I'll let you take her down."

"Yeah, it's still a long flight," Ryland said studying the islands below. It was a stunning view of the area.

"I love the islands here. Sometimes I just wonder about the benefit of, you know, crashing into the sea, coming up on a deserted island, and finding the simple life again," Bullard said with a laugh.

"I hear you," Ryland said. "Every once in a while, I wonder the same."

Several hours later Ryland looked up and said abruptly, "We've made good time considering we've already passed Fiji."

Bullard yawned.

"Let's switch."

Bullard smiled, nodded, and said, "Fine. I'll hand it over to you."

Just then a funny noise came from the engine on the right side.

They looked at each other, and Ryland said, "Uh-oh. That's not good news."

Boom!

And the plane exploded.

Find Bullard's Battle (Book #1) here!

To find out more visit Dale Mayer's website.

smarturl.it/DMSRyland

Damon's Deal: Terkel's Team (Book #1)

Welcome to a brand-new connected series of intrigue, betrayal, and … murder, from the *USA Today* best-selling author Dale Mayer. A series with all the elements you've come to love, plus so much more… including psychics!

A betrayal from within has Terkel frantic to protect those he can, as his team falls one by one, from a murderous killer he helped create.

ICE POURED HERSELF a coffee and sat down at the compound's massive dining room table with the others. When her phone rang, she smiled at the number displayed. "Hey, Terk. How're you doing?" She put the call on Speakerphone.

"I'm okay," Terkel said, his voice distracted and tight.

"Terk?" Merk called from across the table. He got up and walked closer and sat across from Levi. "You don't sound too good, brother. What's up?"

"I'm fine," Terk said. "Or I will be. Right now, things are blown to shit."

"As in literally?" Merk asked.

"The entire group," Terk said, "they're all gone. I had a solid team of eight, and they're all gone."

"Dead?"

Several others stood to join them, gathered around Ice's phone. Levi stepped forward, his hand on Ice's shoulder. "Terk? Are they all dead?"

"No." Terk took a deep breath. "I'm not making sense. I'm sorry."

"Take it easy," Ice said, her voice calm and reassuring. "What do you mean, *they're all gone?*"

"All their abilities are gone," he said. "Something's happened to them. Somebody has deliberately removed whatever super senses they could utilize—or what we have been utilizing for the last ten years for the government." His tone was bitter. "When the US gov recently closed us down, they promised that our black ops department would never rise again, but I didn't expect them to attack us personally."

"What are you talking about?" Merk said in alarm, standing up now to stare at Ice's phone. "Are you in danger?"

"Maybe? I don't know," Terk said. "I need to find out exactly what the hell's going on."

"What can we do to help?" Ice asked.

Terk gave a broken laugh. "That's not why I'm calling. Well, it is, but it isn't."

Ice looked at Merk, who frowned, as he shook his head. Ice knew he and the others had heard Terk's stressed out tone and the completely confusing bits and pieces coming from his mouth. Ice said, "Terk, you're not making sense again. Take a breath and explain. Please. You're scaring me."

Terk took a long slow deep breath. "Tell Stone to open the gate," he said. "She's out there."

"Who's out there?" Levi asked, hopped up, looked outside, and shrugged.

"She's coming up the road now. You have to let her in."

"Who? Why?"

"*Because*," he said, "she's also harnessed with C-4."

"Jesus," Levi said, bolting to display the camera feeds to the big screen in the room. "Is it live?"

"It is, and she's been sent to you."

"Well, that's an interesting move," Ice said, her voice sharp, activating her comm to connect to Stone in the control room. "Who's after us?"

"I think it's rebels within the Iranian government. But it could be our own government. I don't know anymore," Terk snapped. "I also don't know how they got her so close to you. Or how they pinned your connection to me," he said. "I've been very careful."

"We can look after ourselves," Ice said immediately. "But who is this woman to you?"

"She's pregnant," he said, "so that adds to the intensity here."

"Understood. So who is the father? Is he connected somehow?"

There was silence on the other end.

Merk said, "Terk, talk to us."

"She's carrying my baby," Terk replied, his voice heavy.

Merk, his expression grim, looked at Ice, her face mirroring his shock. He asked, "How do you know her, Terk?"

"Brother, you don't understand," Terk said. "I've never met this woman before in my life." And, with that, the phone went dead.

Find Terkel's Team (Book #1) here!

To find out more visit Dale Mayer's website.

smarturl.it/DMSTTDamon

Author's Note

Thank you for reading Johan's Joy: Heroes for Hire, Book 21! If you enjoyed the book, please take a moment and leave a short review.

Dear reader,

I love to hear from readers, and you can contact me at my website: www.dalemayer.com or at my Facebook author page. To be informed of new releases and special offers, sign up for my newsletter or follow me on BookBub. And if you are interested in joining Dale Mayer's Reader Group, here is the Facebook sign up page.
https://smarturl.it/DaleMayerFBGroup

Cheers,
Dale Mayer

Your THREE Free Books
Are Waiting!

Grab your copy of SEALs of Honor Books 1 – 3 for free!

Meet Mason, Hawk and Dane. *Brave, badass warriors who serve their country with honor and love their women to the limits of life and death.*

DOWNLOAD your copy right now! Just tell me where to send it.

www.smarturl.it/DaleHonorFreeBundle

About the Author

Dale Mayer is a *USA Today* best-selling author, best known for her SEALs military romances, her Psychic Visions series, and her Lovely Lethal Garden cozy series. Her contemporary romances are raw and full of passion and emotion (Broken But ... Mending series). Her thrillers will keep you guessing (By Death series), and her romantic comedies will keep you giggling (*It's a Dog's Life*, a stand-alone novella; and the Broken Protocols series, starring Charming Marvin, the cat).

Dale honors the stories that come to her—and some of them are crazy and break all the rules and cross multiple genres!

To go with her fiction, she also writes nonfiction in many different fields, with books available on résumé writing, companion gardening, and the US mortgage system. She has recently published her Career Essentials series. All her books are available in print and ebook format.

Connect with Dale Mayer Online

Dale's Website – www.dalemayer.com

Twitter – @DaleMayer

Facebook – facebook.com/DaleMayer.author

BookBub – bookbub.com/authors/dale-mayer

Also by Dale Mayer

Published Adult Books:

Bullard's Battle

Ryland's Reach, Book 1

Cain's Cross, Book 2

Eton's Escape, Book 3

Garret's Gambit, Book 4

Kano's Keep, Book 5

Fallon's Flaw, Book 6

Quinn's Quest, Book 7

Bullard's Beauty, Book 8

Bullard's Best, Book 9

Terkel's Team

Damon's Deal, Book 1

Kate Morgan

Simon Says... Hide, Book 1

Hathaway House

Aaron, Book 1

Brock, Book 2

Cole, Book 3

Denton, Book 4

The K9 Files

Harley, Book 14

The K9 Files, Books 1–2

The K9 Files, Books 3–4

The K9 Files, Books 5–6

The K9 Files, Books 7–8

The K9 Files, Books 9–10

The K9 Files, Books 11–12

Lovely Lethal Gardens

Arsenic in the Azaleas, Book 1

Bones in the Begonias, Book 2

Corpse in the Carnations, Book 3

Daggers in the Dahlias, Book 4

Evidence in the Echinacea, Book 5

Footprints in the Ferns, Book 6

Gun in the Gardenias, Book 7

Handcuffs in the Heather, Book 8

Ice Pick in the Ivy, Book 9

Jewels in the Juniper, Book 10

Killer in the Kiwis, Book 11

Lifeless in the Lilies, Book 12

Murder in the Marigolds, Book 13

Lovely Lethal Gardens, Books 1–2

Lovely Lethal Gardens, Books 3–4

Lovely Lethal Gardens, Books 5–6

Lovely Lethal Gardens, Books 7–8

Lovely Lethal Gardens, Books 9–10

Psychic Vision Series

Tuesday's Child

Hide 'n Go Seek

Maddy's Floor

Garden of Sorrow

Knock Knock...

Rare Find

Eyes to the Soul

Now You See Her

Shattered

Into the Abyss

Seeds of Malice

Eye of the Falcon

Itsy-Bitsy Spider

Unmasked

Deep Beneath

From the Ashes

Stroke of Death

Ice Maiden

Snap, Crackle...

Psychic Visions Books 1–3

Psychic Visions Books 4–6

Psychic Visions Books 7–9

By Death Series

Touched by Death

Haunted by Death

Chilled by Death

By Death Books 1–3

Broken Protocols – Romantic Comedy Series

Cat's Meow

Cat's Pajamas

Cat's Cradle

Cat's Claus

Broken Protocols 1-4

Broken and... Mending

Skin

Scars

Scales (of Justice)

Broken but... Mending 1-3

Glory

Genesis

Tori

Celeste

Glory Trilogy

Biker Blues

Morgan: Biker Blues, Volume 1

Cash: Biker Blues, Volume 2

SEALs of Honor

Mason: SEALs of Honor, Book 1

Hawk: SEALs of Honor, Book 2

Dane: SEALs of Honor, Book 3

Swede: SEALs of Honor, Book 4

Shadow: SEALs of Honor, Book 5

Cooper: SEALs of Honor, Book 6

Heroes for Hire

SEALs of Steel

The Mavericks

Diesel, Book 13

Jerricho, Book 14

The Mavericks, Books 1–2

The Mavericks, Books 3–4

The Mavericks, Books 5–6

The Mavericks, Books 7–8

The Mavericks, Books 9–10

The Mavericks, Books 11–12

Collections

Dare to Be You...

Dare to Love...

Dare to be Strong...

RomanceX3

Standalone Novellas

It's a Dog's Life

Riana's Revenge

Second Chances

Published Young Adult Books:

Family Blood Ties Series

Vampire in Denial

Vampire in Distress

Vampire in Design

Vampire in Deceit

Vampire in Defiance

Vampire in Conflict

Vampire in Chaos

Vampire in Crisis

Vampire in Control

Vampire in Charge

Family Blood Ties Set 1–3

Family Blood Ties Set 1–5

Family Blood Ties Set 4–6

Family Blood Ties Set 7–9

Sian's Solution, A Family Blood Ties Series Prequel Novelette

Design series

Dangerous Designs

Deadly Designs

Darkest Designs

Design Series Trilogy

Standalone

In Cassie's Corner

Gem Stone (a Gemma Stone Mystery)

Time Thieves

Published Non-Fiction Books:

Career Essentials

Career Essentials: The Résumé

Career Essentials: The Cover Letter

Career Essentials: The Interview

Career Essentials: 3 in 1